Marji's Books

The Christmas Tree Treasure Hunt

Grime Fighter Series

Grime Beat

Grime Wave

Grime Spree

Grime Family

Grime & Punishment

Heath's Point Suspense

Counter Point

Breaking Point

Boiling Point (coming soon)

Flash Point (coming soon)

Dallas Duets Clean Billionaire Romance

Ain't Misbehaving

Cry Me a River (coming soon)

Puttin' on the Ritz (coming soon)

Grime Wave

**Grime Fighter Mystery
Book #2**

Marji Laine

Grime Wave
Second Edition
© 2019 Marji Laine
ISBN: 978-1-944120-92-4

This book is a work of fiction. Names, characters, places, and incidents are either products of the author's imagination or used fictitiously. Any similarity to actual people and/or events is purely coincidental.

Faith Driven Book Production Services
Find out more about the author: *Marji Laine.com*
Or email her at: *AuthorMarjiLaine@gmail.com*

Printed in the United States of America.

All of my family support my writing career,
so it's difficult to choose
one person for my dedication.
However, for this book, I choose
my oldest daughter.

Katie
Steady, Compassionate
Singing, Laughing, Loving
Focused on Following Christ
Inspiring
I'm so awed at how the Lord blesses.
And this lady is such an amazing blessing to
everyone who knows her!

*"Now to Him who is able to do far
more abundantly beyond all that we
ask or think, according to the power
that works within us, to Him be the
glory in the church and in Christ Jesus
to all generations forever and ever.
Amen." Ephesians 3:20-21*

Chapter One

"I didn't giggle." Dani Foster shouldered her purse while her friend fussed with the key in the office door.

"Yes, you did." Carla retracted the bolt and let Dani inside first. "Sounded just like a teenager heading for prom."

Stuff and nonsense. She made for the bathroom. "I only said my hair could use a little help after being stuck in the helmet all day." She pushed open the door. "Don't you want to primp?"

Carla let out a trill of laughter. Now *that* was a giggle. "I married my man. Don't have to impress him anymore." She laughed again and headed for the entrance next to a marble-topped counter in front of a stone facade. "I'll get my phone and meet you back here."

Her phone. The excuse to come by her office, but it was more likely Carla's attempt to calm Dani's nerves about this first official date with Jay. She stared at the mirror and fluffed her hair.

It had taken long enough to get to this point. February was a brutal month for suicides. Her dad had taught her that. If Jay's schedule had been anything like hers, he'd barely had time for a shower.

She applied a little lipstick and brushed on gloss over it. Too much. Made her look like a prom-bound teenager in addition to simply sounding like one. A paper towel dispensed with the gloss. She touched up the color and surveyed herself. Not too bad. Her makeup had held. No stray mascara. Her long hair still had some curl to the bangs, waves and body throughout.

Tucking a stray strand behind her ear, she spritzed some perfume, shoved it and her lipstick back inside her purse, then pulled open the door. "I'm ready as I'll ever be." A curl of anticipation crawled through her insides. Nerves. Good grief. Now she *felt* like an adolescent.

"Carla, did you find your phone?" She paused at the opening and listened for a response. Nothing.

"We don't want to be too late." A lousy way to start any date, but especially a first one, and after over a month of trying to fit it in.

She walked down a makeshift hallway with a wall on her left and a cubicle matrix on her right. "Are you still back here?" She glanced into the first cube. One bare desk and the other cluttered with photos and children's art along with notepads, empty file folders, and an *I Love My Mama* coffee mug.

The silence of the empty room flinched when a noisy heater kicked on. The back of Dani's neck prickled. "Carla?" Her voice took on a soft, squeaky texture. Where was that woman?

The last time Dani had worried about a friend, her roommate Tasha had been kidnapped. But such couldn't be the case this time. Dani had only been in the bathroom ten minutes, max.

A muffled sound came from behind her, farther into the maze. Hard to say if it was a cry or an answer. Dani moved in that direction and started to call again but halted. Being a detective's daughter brought the caution out in her. Why advertise where she was? Especially if there was a reason for the knot tightening around her middle.

She peeked into the next cube on her right but saw no one and took another step. *Wait a minute.* She poked her head back around the opening.

A tiny rivulet of reddish-brown seeped under the gap of the false wall opposite her. Blood?

"Carla!" With both hands, she pushed against the edge of the wall and propelled herself around the corner to where the liquid had to originate.

Her friend knelt, rather bowed, barely inside

the entrance. Dani gasped and dropped to her knees behind her. "Are you hurt?" Her back and head didn't show signs of blood. "*Where* are you hurt? How?" Images from her horror half a year ago— half a life ago—flooded her mind. Her stomach recoiled at the vision and her muscles stiffened for a second.

But that had been a hopeless situation last summer. Well before her arrival in Dallas. And it had nothing to do with her friend.

Carla was still breathing. Still upright. Dani braced her friend's shoulder with one hand and felt for a pulse on her neck.

Then she saw the source of the blood. A man lay on his side, his back against the partition.

"Albert Theisen." Carla's voice sounded oddly detached.

Dani glanced at the nameplate on the desk to her left. She leaned toward it. Surely there was something to put pressure on the wound. Scattered file folders covered the surface. The top drawer hung open, revealing nothing except black pens, a roll of TUMS, and a bright orange toothpick. No help at all.

"I couldn't get the bleeding to stop." Carla raised her reddened hands. Large blotches stained the cream-colored wool of her suit jacket from cuffs to elbows.

Dani looked back at the man. Deep crimson coated the front of what appeared to be a light-yellow shirt. His tie hung over his shoulder, probably flung there when the man fell.

"Come away." She gave a slight tug on her friend's shoulders. They didn't need to be in a position to ruin any evidence.

Carla stood abruptly, causing Dani to teeter and fall onto her behind.

"I should phone the police." Carla started to reach toward the desk.

Dani held up her hand. "No, don't touch anything. We can use my cell phone." She pushed to her feet and leaned back down over the man's face. His eyes closed, he might have been sleeping, if not for the morbid decoration on his shirt front. She checked for a pulse at the flaccid neck of the very dead man. Nothing except cooling skin, as she expected.

She shoved her friend along the walkway and back into the reception area. Pulling her phone from her shoulder bag, she helped Carla into an armchair then dialed 9-1-1. While she answered the operator's questions, she kept a hand on her friend's shoulder in case she became unsteady.

The knees of her friend's light blue slacks had streaks in the same rusty color as her jacket. Only her heavily appliqued blouse seemed to have escaped the mess, although with such a vibrant design, no one would be able to tell. Tears rimmed the bottom lids of Carla's large, dark eyes. Her flawless creamed-coffee skin no longer held her usual model-like quality as it had taken on a pallor across her high cheekbones and an ashy look to the hollows beneath them.

"Let's get you cleaned up a little." Dani led Carla to the bathroom and helped her out of her jacket.

Carla washed her hands clean, but the redness in her eyes didn't quite disappear. "He was one of the associates. Trying to rebuild his life after an ugly divorce."

Dani handed her a paper towel and opened the door. Returning to the entry, Carla once again sat on the couch, her eyes fixed on a large mosaic vase on a glass end table across from her.

Dani squatted next to her. "Were you friends?"

She nodded. "He was a nice man. Had a couple of boys, his wife's kids."

"Does she live in town?" A messy divorce sure offered a prime motive.

"I heard she was heading for Los Angeles, but I don't think she's left yet."

"So his wife was married before?"

Carla blew her nose. "Not sure, but after almost four years, Albert found out that she and the kids' father were still seeing each other."

"That's terrible. Poor guy."

She straightened and pierced Dani with a wide-eyed look. "Could she have done this? His wife?"

Dani stood. "Yeah, that was my thought. But if she's with another guy ..."

"She failed to get any money, though. Albert was a good salesman and a smart investor."

"Loaded?" That made a good motive.

Carla nodded. "And the wife didn't get a penny. Albert was even meeting with his attorney next week."

"Cutting her out of his will?"

"And setting up a trust for the two kids. He really cared about those boys."

"Good man."

"Though I never saw anything that hinted of reciprocation. No Father's Day cards or birthday stuff." She sniffed and crossed one leg over the other. "He didn't deserve this."

Seeing a tear fall, Dani rushed to the ladies'

room and collected a small wad of toilet paper. She handed it to Carla and dialed her phone. "I'm calling Tyrone."

She choked on a sob. "Tell him I'm all right. I don't want him to worry."

Dani hesitated. Maybe calling Jay would be a better choice? They would likely be waiting at the theater by now. He would be the more level-headed of the two. She punched his contact link.

He answered before it even had a chance to ring. "Where are you?" Tension played through his low voice.

"Ingersol, Lynman, and Kash, remember? Carla had to stop and get her phone." A siren wailed on his end. "Where are you?"

"Coming your way." He said something off the speaker.

"You're coming here?"

"I got the call. You two are both okay?"

"Yes. One of Carla's co-workers...."

"Say no more. You'll need to give an official

statement."

Official … what? "I called you because I need to talk to a friend."

"I can't play that role. Not now. I don't want to even hear what you have to say until after you speak to a detective."

She huffed. "Are you telling me I should've called someone else?" Tyrone would've been a better choice after all.

"I told you. I'm on this case. I have to follow protocol. That means you give your report to someone else, first. I can't discuss it. I don't want to influence you in any way."

"Insufferable." *Oops*. She hadn't meant to say that aloud. "Fine." Hopefully she followed up quickly enough.

"Dani, please understand."

His compassionate tone gave her an instant stab of guilt. "It's okay." She rang off. What a self-absorbed whiner she was. *God, please bless Jay as he drives.*

She knelt next to Carla. "Tyrone's on his way. Jay got the call."

"I bet Ty is a basket case. Both of them." She sniffed. "Jay really likes you, you know."

"Mm-hmm. That's why we've spent so much time together." It was supposed to sound like a joke, but her words came out more doubtful than she'd intended.

"Ty says he comes to all of the scenes y'all work for him."

"He always did that. To make sure he hadn't missed anything important."

"But now he comes and talks to y'all in person. He doesn't have to do that. And he hasn't really had the time." She dabbed at her eyes with the wad of tissue. "He's taking every opportunity to spend time with you, sugar. Even if it's only a half hour every few days."

She *had* seen him more often since their excitement back in January. She'd even begun to look for him at the job sites. "Well, they're better off now, knowing we're fine."

Carla lifted her eyes to the ceiling. "Fine is relative." She held out the disintegrated ball of tissue. "Could I get some more?"

"Sure." Moving felt good, especially with a helpful purpose. She stood and headed for the bathroom.

"Honey, what did you get all over yourself?"

Dani halted as Carla reached to give her hip a swat. Half-turning toward the windows, Dani arched and stared in the tinted reflection of the glass at her backside. Her navy slacks were covered with something whitish. She brushed her rump.

"Where in the world did you find dust?" Carla rubbed her fingers together. "Face powder?"

"I'm glad it isn't paint." Dani knocked off another layer.

Carla examined her own derriere in the glass. "Where did it come from?" She pounded the cloth cushion on the couch a few times with the flat of her hand before sitting back down.

Before Dani could answer, whirling red and blue lights tracked across the front of the room. Two cruisers pulled in with Jay's gray-black Charger close behind.

She darted a look at Carla. "You going to be all right?"

The woman nodded then lifted her pointer finger and gestured for her to turn around.

Dani pivoted once more. "All the dust gone now?"

Her friend nodded. "If only *all* of this mess could be cleaned up so easily."

Chapter Two

Jay Hunter followed two cruisers into the lot. Good thing he'd spoken to Dani. Though it hadn't calmed Tyrone too much. "There's your wife. See? She's fine."

Carla sat on a couch, and Dani stood nearby.

Tyrone unlatched his belt and bolted from his door as Jay braked. "Hey, wait."

His friend could have saved his energy … and his knee, still-recovering from that gun-shot. One of the uniforms ahead of them stopped Ty at the front door.

"That's my wife in there." His shouting wasn't

going to get him any help.

Jay shoved the car into park. Ty's rant left reason behind and was likely going to land him in the back of a cruiser. Maybe that would be for the best. Get him out of the way.

Irritable thought. He blew out an exhale and turned off the ignition. What a lousy friend he'd become. To Ty and to Dani.

Her voice over the phone had sounded more rattled than he had expected, considering her job. But then, an actual body wasn't something she usually dealt with. Not that he'd comforted her at all.

Thank You, God, for protecting my ... for protecting her. Dani wasn't his anything. And wouldn't be if they couldn't spend quality time together. He popped his trunk and removed the cases with his gear and tools.

This date was a certain bust.

Just another crime scene. Like his partner always said. This time it drew him from his pity-party. Then, the man himself arrived. Before Jay could shove his trunk closed, Cal's silver Taurus halted next to him.

"Got the laser scanner?" Cal climbed from the Ford and visited his backseat for a load of his own.

"Yep." Their newest tool, or toy as his partner referred to it.

Jay followed the veteran investigator through the glass doors, ignored a uniformed cop's directions, and glanced at Dani.

She leveled her chocolate gaze on him. A crevice split the area between her arched brows where her brown bangs framed her forehead.

He should stop. Speak. Something.

He lifted his chin and held her gaze a moment. That was the best he could do with officers coming between them and the detective team due at any moment.

As he passed into a modified hallway, she disappeared from sight. His face heated. Good thing they'd enjoyed one unofficial date, albeit a blind one. After he just left her sitting there, she might not offer him a second chance.

"Watch yourself." Cal's warning and abrupt halt indicated the crime scene. Jay peeked around the corner at the man sprawled face up on the floor. The nearest desk was cluttered with files, but the far one held a glossy of Tyrone and Carla. A wedding picture from the looks of it.

This kept getting better.

Jay set his case down and carried the scanner to the center of the space. He stretched out the tripod and checked the focus and lighting before setting the timer and retracing his steps.

As the machine started its soft whirring, he retracted a pair of gloves from a package in his bag and snapped them on his hands. "Not much blood."

"Yeah, but did you notice all the stains on the clothes of that woman out there?"

Cal must have meant Carla. Jay would have noticed something like that on Dani. Funny how he didn't even remember noticing Carla as he passed through the room. "That woman is Tyrone Reid's wife."

The man lifted his eyebrow. "Really. Well, looks like your gal is holding up all right. You wanna go talk to her while this thing runs?" Cal pulled a toothpick from his mouth and tucked it into his pocket before donning a set of gloves.

"Want to—yes. But not until she's signed off on her story."

"You're such a do-gooder. You think she had something to do with that guy's death?"

"Of course not." How could he imagine such?

"Well, your unwillingness to talk to her, even give her a thumbs up, sure screams that you think she's done something wrong." He shook his head. "And here, I thought you had feelings for this gal."

How did he know that? "I never said anything about feelings. I mean … I care about her." He shrugged. "She's a friend." And if he'd had only one empty evening this last month, she'd likely be more than that by now.

"Then get out there and tell your friend you've got her back. We have to wait for the scan to finish anyway." Cal stared at him. Almost like a dare.

His partner was right. Normal, when it came to matters of police work. With women, not so much.

Jay nodded and made for the front of the building. He yanked off his gloves and shoved them into his pocket. Even if he were putting his possible promotion in jeopardy by speaking to her out of order, he owed her some compassion. Especially after he had shut her down on the phone.

Seemed like just being around her put his future in danger, in more ways than one. How could he know the woman for less than half a year and find her involved in not one but two crimes already? Not that the first one was in any way her fault. Or this one either, for that matter.

He hoped.

Dani stood alone near the darkened windows in the corner. Perriman and Durwood had arrived. They both spoke to Carla. She seemed to have regained her normal coloring from when he'd seen her from his car. No sign of Tyrone, but the tinted glass masked the waning light outside.

He strolled toward the beautiful brunette. Dani turned in his direction as he drew near.

"You all right?"

She lifted one corner of her generous mouth. "This is all horrific."

He gave her a one-armed hug. Not the way he wanted to embrace and comfort her, but the best he could do under the circumstances. In fact, more than he should be doing. "Have you already given a statement?"

She nodded.

Good. At least he couldn't be accused of undue influence. "Carla looks to be doing fine."

"She's amazing. She told me the victim, Albert, finished with a brutal divorce last week. I'd look at the ex-wife and her boyfriend, if I were you."

Her advice edged too close to his comfort line.

"Did you tell the others about that?"

"Of course. You think I'd hide something so important?" She pulled away.

"No. But I don't want to be privy to anything you may have forgotten about when you spoke to the detectives." This narrow margin between cop and boyfriend—or at least friend—felt like one of the beams of a skyscraper.

"I'm sorry. I'm still upset." She closed the gap between them again. "I'll have to get over it, though. Chances are we'll be cleaning this up tomorrow or the next day, I guess."

He ached to slide his arm around her shoulders. Instead, he stuck his hand into his pocket. "Kellerman's Trauma and Crisis Cleaners always gets my vote." He smiled. "And you're dealing with this fine. Even considering what you do for a living."

"I don't deal with dead people. Only the mess they leave behind."

"And brilliantly." He gave her a half-smile and

laid his hand against her arm. "Cal's probably waiting for me by now, though. When they say you can go, call me."

"Okay." She locked eyes with him. "I'm sorry about our date."

A section of bangs chose that moment to detach and topple over her forehead. Adorable.

He stroked the hair away from her face, tucking it behind her ear as his smile spread. How could he suppress one, facing such a cute look? "We'll set it up again. Not to worry."

He turned but looked back as he reached the opening to the other room. She was watching him. He lifted his hand then headed down the hallway.

Ugh. How this woman twisted up his insides. He was at a murder scene for pity's sake. Lord, please straighten out my thoughts, so I can do my job to the best of my ability.

He met up with Cal again inside the cube. The laser had completed its task.

"Hope this view is as good as the last two." Cal

removed the scanner from the tripod. Only the third time they had used it, they still had to follow up with their normal collection of data and measurements. At least until the new technology confirmed its reliability.

Dr. Konn pushed into the small space. "I guess the party's here." He smacked Jay on the back as he passed and set his bag on the floor. "Two more days 'til spring training."

"You going to Surprise?" Jay talked Texas Rangers with the man all year long, but March was special.

"Got a couple of weekends set aside, if I can get away." He squatted near the body and slipped latex gloves over his hands.

"No one can call you in during your off-duty hours if you're in Arizona."

"True enough." He laughed and touched the thick neck of the victim. "This guy's not been gone too long."

"You're slipping, Doc. You haven't run your

tests yet." Cal stretched out his measuring tape between the wall and the chair.

"Don't worry. I'll be as thorough as I ever am. How long have you been here? Half hour?" Konn glanced from Jay to Cal and back.

"A little less." Maybe twenty minutes since he and Cal had actually arrived on the scene.

The doctor felt the man's neck again. "I'll check the liver, but I don't think he's been gone more than a half hour. Those women in the other room—they found him?"

Jay's face heated. "Yes." Maybe Dani had been in danger after all.

Konn pulled a scalpel from his bag. "I wouldn't let them go far." He made a tiny cut through the victim's abdomen before exchanging the scalpel for a long, slender thermometer with a pointed edge. "I think you've got your killers right there, but I'll know better when I finish my tests."

His words might just as well have been a bucket of ice water.

Chapter Three

Was this a nightmare? Dani crossed the asphalt to a police cruiser. Déjà vu of the worst kind. A female officer opened the back door. At least they'd left her un-cuffed this time.

"What do you mean we need to come with you?" Carla's voice sounded shrill. Another officer had her by the elbow, propelling her across the lot to a different car. She looked ready to fight, and no wonder. They'd been waiting for almost two hours to be allowed to leave. Now the officers wanted to load them up and take them to the station.

Dani climbed in. "I don't understand. Am I

under arrest?"

The officer closed the door behind her, then she opened the front door and stood next to it. "No, ma'am. But you'll need to answer some questions."

"Didn't I already do that?"

"The detectives need to go over a few things again before they can release you."

"So I am under arrest?" It sure sounded like it.

"Not at present."

Okay. She stared at the doorway to the room of cubes. Did Jay know anything about this? "May I make a phone call?"

The woman turned and eyed her cell phone. "There's no need for a lawyer. Unless you have something to hide." She narrowed her gaze.

Boy, did she have things to hide. Relaxing her face muscles, she painted on a stoic calm. "No, only a friend."

The woman didn't exactly nod, but she looked away.

Dani stroked the screen until Jay's face

appeared. Deeply tanned from his Native American roots, and with a hint of his half-smile along his smooth jaw. She'd been with a handsome man before. The thought sickened her.

Jay's compassion, the light in his brown eyes and the kindness he showed drew her more than his muscles and classic good looks. Although they were still a big plus.

Her finger hovered over the connect button for a moment. Then she sighed. As much as she wished for his comfort, he wasn't her protector.

She dialed Matthew Donaldson's number instead. It was late. Again. Why did she always call her witness security agent after hours? Not that it mattered. He'd fuss no matter when she called.

"What is it this time, Ms. Foster? A cat scratched your window, or another car backfired outside your apartment?" His bland voice held no interest. In fact, he sounded like he wanted to take her pizza order.

Boy, he was going to have her head over this.

"Neither. I'm being taken to the police department for questioning."

"What?"

She pulled the phone away for a moment, allowing for his outburst.

"What have you done?"

"Nothing. I mean it. My friend left her phone at her office. We went back to get it, and she found the body of a coworker lying in the cube they shared." How could anyone think she'd done anything wrong with that?

And yet, the police were insisting she go back to the station.

A couple of plain-clothes cops came through the reception area pushing a gurney with a body bag strapped to it. Dani shuddered. The look of death on the man's face would revisit her dreams.

"Are you listening to me?" Matthew's voice called her back from the image.

Not exactly. "I'm still here."

"Say nothing. Don't even give your name,

though you may not have to."

"I already have. They've been questioning my friend and me for a couple of hours already." Well, more making them wait around than actually answering questions.

Something like a tornadic gale blew through the phone. "Say no more, then. I'll get to work on this." The phone went silent.

She'd always suspected Matthew of being full of hot air.

The officer closed her door, leaving Dani isolated. How long could they keep her in here?

A man with a medical bag came through, chatting with the fellow behind him. Dani recognized one of the men from Jay's team. He carried a black bag, like a tackle box on steroids. Jay emerged behind them with a duffel in one hand and a tripod in the other.

Oh, he looked good. She sucked in air and blew it out. Exiting the building, he glanced at her Honda first then scanned the lot until his eyes met hers. He advanced toward the officer still standing near the front of the cruiser. His manner was entirely too calm. Where was his outrage at his friends being hauled off like crooks? He said something to the woman, and she answered before he moved on to the trunk of his Charger.

Wait. Didn't he care? Wasn't he going to say anything to her? What kind of hero walks away like that?

Her driver got in at that moment. She followed the car carrying Carla.

Arriving at the station, Dani was directed to her favorite little bench. If she had to sit as long as she'd been forced to in January, she might carve her initials.

Carla flounced in after her. "Are you all right?"

"I'm fine. Bored and bummed that I have to sit here again."

Tyrone came in, cuffed and led by an officer. "Baby."

The cop pointed to a seat. "If you'll calm

down, I'll take those off."

The big man nodded, but his anger-charged eyes glared at the cop.

"You were arrested?"

"Technically, detained." The officer unlocked the cuffs, and Tyrone wrapped his arms around his wife.

"Stay here until you're called." The cop pocketed the metal rings and sauntered down a hallway.

Still clinging to Carla, Ty looked across to Dani. "You all right?"

"Been better, but I'm okay."

"This is crazy, bringing us in here." Carla's voice rang with indignation.

One of the men from the site wandered over. A little on the paunchy side, he had a receding hairline and a toothpick lodged between his teeth. "Actually, because you're friends of Hunter, you're being allowed to stay together."

Tyrone lifted his head. "I've seen you before."

"I'm Jay's partner. Cutter's the name. Your company does good work."

He shook Cutter's hand. "So does your team."

"Not my team. Jay's the wonder boy." He loosened the knot in his green shamrock tie. "This is a serious situation. The detectives have to be sure of the facts before they release anyone. Even a close friend."

Tyrone didn't respond, but his eyes told the story of all the thoughts he held inside. And his normal wide smile had abandoned his smooth, brown face.

"Nice to meet you folks." Cutter strolled back around a corner, the way he'd come.

His words settled like old mayonnaise in her stomach. Would they have to stay there all night? She kept to her corner of the bench while Carla and Ty talked softly on their side.

Carla had aged. The pallor she'd worn at the office had returned. That with her weariness of what they'd already been through that evening gave her an extra decade she didn't deserve.

Before too long, a detective came over. Durwood-something, or maybe it was something-Durwood. He asked Tyrone to stay where he was while he escorted Carla down a hall.

The big man fidgeted and shifted in his seat. His concern touched Dani. This was the way a man cared about a woman.

She grabbed hold of his hand. "Lord, we're feeling attacked right now." She leaned close, with her words barely above a whisper. "Please give us Your peace. Let Your truth prevail over every cranny of the investigation. Cover Tyrone and especially Carla with confidence and courage."

When she said her amen, her friend squeezed her hand. "You're the real thing, Dani."

His words shamed her. She wasn't even a real Dani. But the time for that revelation might never come.

A few minutes later, a guy in a suit with a name-badge dangling from his lapel came calling her name. She glanced around for a glimpse of Jay, but he never showed. Had he even returned?

She followed the stocky fellow to a small office. Another man sat behind a desk labeled Capt. Madison. He stood but didn't smile when she arrived. After introducing himself, he indicated a chair. Then, he moved to the windowed wall, which opened out to the desks that filled the rest of the office, and snapped the blinds shut on each one.

He returned to his desk and picked up a folder. "You're in the witness protection program?"

What did she do now? She glanced from him to the man who had brought her here. How could she answer that?

Captain Madison handed her the receiver of a phone.

"Hello?"

"You are to answer them, yes." Matthew's voice.

"Are you sure?" Would this mean another move for her?

"Say it, Dani, and hand the phone back to the captain."

She handed the phone to the suited, graying man. "Yes."

The captain clicked the receiver into an old-fashioned intercom.

"All right, Mr. Donaldson. As we question your witness, call out with anything that concerns you." Captain Madison turned a glare in Dani's direction. "Does anyone besides your agent know of your background?"

"Wait." Matthew's voice sputtered from the speaker. "I don't see how that has any bearing on your case."

"She's found at the scene of a murder. The possibility that someone is trying to kill her comes into play, don't you think?" The captain might have been speaking to Matthew, but he stared at Dani. His eyes hardened as he crossed his arms.

"I assure you there is no connection." Matthew had control over this situation. Why did Dani even have to be there?

The captain's scowl deepened. "Frankly, Mr. Donaldson, your assurance doesn't mean anything. You know nothing of the dead man or the circumstances of the murder."

"Then why don't you enlighten me?"

"All I want to know is if anyone else in town knows about her background. If the answer is no, we can eliminate that avenue."

Silence grew on Matthew's end while the captain continued to stare at Dani. She looked at her hands, clasped in her lap.

"I can't answer that." Matthew's volume lowered. "But Dani can to the best of her ability."

Wait, what? He acted like he'd handle everything, then he whipped that tightrope right out from under her. Why? Did he think she'd been mouthing off?

She straightened and faced the captain. "No one knows about me, as far as I'm aware."

"And you didn't know the dead man."

"I'd never seen him before."

The captain hammered her with questions, forcing her back through the experience. She found Carla with the body. She checked for a pulse. She and Carla left for the reception area. They stayed there until the police came. End of story. Only she had to go over it again and again.

Finally, Captain Madison addressed Matthew again. "All right. We'll agree to your demands."

"What demands?" Oof. Why did she always open her big mouth?

"I'll take care of this." Matthew went into discussion with the chief about how to remove indications that she'd ever been there. "So the only record of her involvement in this situation is in your head, Captain. Yours and whomever you have taking notes."

"Officer Gutierrez, sir." The man who had escorted her had taken silent residence in the corner of the room until that moment.

"And the notes?" Matthew left the question

hanging.

Gutierrez ripped the top page from his notepad out and balled it up loudly. "Discarded, Sir."

"Perfect. Thank you, Captain."

Captain Madison's scowl deepened.

"Dani, I expect to hear nothing more from you for the next several months. Understood?" Matthew's demand sounded like business as usual.

"I suppose if my life is in danger I should send you an email?"

"You know what I mean. No more playing around. Stay out of trouble."

Like she'd put herself in this position. She clamped her back teeth against the retort she ached to throw. Instead, she looked at Madison. "Am I free to go?"

He lowered to his chair and raised his eyebrows without letting his gaze wander from her face.

She took that as a yes and scooted from the room.

Jay was leaning against a desk outside the door. He straightened when she came out. "Grueling?"

"Annoying." But it was so good to find him there waiting. Especially after she'd felt so abandoned with Matthew as her only support. "I'm glad you're not ashamed to be seen with me."

"Of course not." He ushered her down the hall and fell into step beside her. "But I couldn't interfere. I hope you understand that. Besides, I wasn't worried about you."

Hmm. His explanation seemed logical, though it lacked the defender attitude she'd prefer. "Have they finished with Carla?"

He nodded. "She and Tyrone left a little while ago with the cop who brought him in." He touched her back with one hand and pushed open the door with the other. "Can I take you home?"

Even that slight touch shot sparks through her. "Please." She shoved down the emotion. This wasn't anything romantic, only a polite gentleman willing to transport a stranded person. Like a bus driver or a cabby.

As much as she wanted to relish their first moments alone in over a month, Jay's presence posed a problem. Captain Madison and Officer Gutierrez weren't the only cops who knew she was involved in this murder. But Matthew didn't know anything about Jay.

Dani wasn't ready for that confrontation. Talk about a nightmare. But what if Jay noticed her name missing from the reports?

Chapter Four

The silence in Jay's Charger grew as thick as the smell of his regular morning coffee.

"I'm sorry you had to go through all of that." Sounded lame, but the best he could offer. "Detective work can be tedious sometimes, even for the cops. And especially for the … witnesses." He veered away from the term suspects at the last second. That woulda been a train wreck.

"None of that was your fault."

"Yours either." He turned onto a main artery. "I'll reschedule with Tyrone and Carla." With the Reids along, the conversation was bound to be lively.

"I'd like that." She stroked the surface of her colorless fingernail.

A shame the Reids weren't with them now. A distraction would be a blessing and keep their minds off the dead man in Carla's office. "Listen, this has been a crazy month, but I should have tried harder to carve out some time."

"It's all right. February is often a month with above average suicides and attempts. And with the ice and intense cold, this one has been worse than most."

Did she just spout official statistics? He glanced at her as he made the turn into her neighborhood. "How do you know that?"

She froze for an instant, staring at her hand. "Doesn't everybody?" She shot him a half-smile. Looked almost … nervous. "Like the high suicide rate in cold, rainy climates?"

Obviously, the stress had set in. Of course, the horror of what she found upset her and would probably continue to impact her emotionally for a while. No one besides a cop would ever expect to happen upon a murder victim.

He was used to the experience. If only he could wipe the images out of her mind. A left turn into her complex brought them to a heavy metal gate across the drive. "I guess the gates and fences help you feel safe." Though a little more light would benefit the parking lot.

She slipped her keycard from her purse and handed it to him. "Yes. No reports of assaults at this complex, though I did hear about a recent theft."

Probably by someone who lived in the community, but he wouldn't say that to her. No need to stir up fear. The gate lumbered open. He followed the make-shift street half-way around the complex to building 14. Better lighting there, near the clubhouse.

He parked on the outskirts of the lot and strolled around the car to open her door. Shame they couldn't have made this a real date. She looked beautiful, even though her navy slacks hid her shapely legs. Her blue and white blouse hugged graceful curves, while her long dark waves gave a waterfall effect around her shoulders and down her back.

But this wasn't a date. This was a tragedy. One that wouldn't end anytime soon if he knew the thoroughness of his department. "You look lovely, by the way."

Her slight smile didn't reach her eyes. Didn't she believe him?

He touched her elbow when they reached the stairs to her apartment. "About what happened tonight …."

"I'd prefer to try to forget about that."

Unlikely possibility. "Chances are, officers will need to speak with you again as they learn more about the crime."

She stared at the wrought-iron rail. "If that's the case, I'll deal with it."

Another car pulled in. The headlights caught

them for a moment, and Jay squinted against the glare. "There's no if to this. You're an essential witness. You can probably expect a call tomorrow."

The curly blonde head of Dani's roommate appeared out of the new vehicle. Jay looked down.

"Don't let me interrupt." She snickered and threaded her way around them.

He caught Dani's eye. "You should tell her. She's bound to hear about it."

She stared at the rail again and reached for it with both hands. "Thanks for bringing me home."

"You want me to go up with you?"

She took a step up. "I'm fine, thanks." She turned away from him.

He'd been dismissed. "Can I call you?"

Smirking, she swung back around. "As Jay or Officer Hunter?"

The light-hearted quip was more serious than it sounded. He shrugged. "Both." He stepped upward, letting his hand glide up the rail behind her.

She locked eyes with him. "I know the cop is part of who you are. I guess, I'd hoped that you … not officially or anything …."

"I should have been more comforting."

"I'm asking too much. You've been very kind."

"Now, maybe. But not at first. Not when you really needed my help."

She dropped her chin.

His neck warmed. "I'm sorry, Dani. Having a lady … someone special, involved in one of my investigations is a new one for me." He stroked the back of her shoulder. "It's a balance. I have a job to do. If I act with partiality, not only does my reputation suffer, but my data will be in question." And when data failed, guilty people went free.

"I'm a hindrance to your reputation?" She leaned away from him.

"No. That's not what I meant." He swung his other hand wide, palm up, then let it fall and against his thigh. He locked his gaze with hers. "You couldn't be." Even if he did get a black mark, she wouldn't be to blame.

"I hope not. I don't want to cause you any problems in your work." Pivoting, she trotted up the final steps. She reached the landing and turned back toward him. "And I'll look forward to your call. Preferably from Jay, but I'll take it from Officer Hunter if I need to. Thanks again for the ride." With a smile, she entered her apartment.

Jay leaned back against the rail. He could call her. She couldn't be too annoyed. But the sooner this case veered away from Dani, the sooner he would have the opportunity to explore a possible relationship with her.

Who'd have thought, after his humiliation on the way to the altar, he'd be the least bit interested in another serious relationship. But it had been years, and those dotted with fix-ups through well-meaning friends. Was he ready to get back into dating?

Jogging back to his car, he made up his mind.

He didn't need matchmakers to set him up with Dani. His heart was already going there on its own.

He returned to his station on the edge of Flag Pole Hill. Funny how the exhaustion he'd felt while waiting outside the captain's office disappeared with the enchanting smile of a beautiful woman.

With his second wind kicking into high gear, he strode through the side entrance and made his way to his desk. Better to focus on the evidence he and the team had collected. The physical data, along with the interviews and reports from the detectives.

He sorted through the paperwork and the digital imagery. Nothing jumped out at him, but by the time he'd reached that far into the data, midnight had come and gone. And so had his energy. He only had a few sheets of information left to peruse, probably Dani's report. He fingered through the file. Standard observations report from the first two officers on the scene, then his and Cal's logged entries that they'd written up while Dani was in the captain's office.

That was all? He re-laid each sheet in the file and read through the headings again. Reflections from all concerned, photos of the scene, scans of the victim's identification, Carla's statement, a few other routine forms, but nothing from Dani.

That sleepiness he'd begun to feel vanished. He walked the file to the western wing. The captain was long gone. A detective whose name escaped him sat at one of the desks tapping on his computer. "You working on the Theisen case?"

"Nah, that's Perriman's." He pointed to a standing file holder. "Put it there, and I'll get it to him."

Jay slid the slender folder into a slot. "Is that all you've got? I mean, I thought I'd find another report included."

"Then the report hasn't been written, yet. You know how it goes." The guy shrugged and continued his pointer-finger dance over his desktop keyboard. "It'll be in the database by morning, though."

With no other recourse, Jay left the building and expended adrenaline running the perimeter of the lot before stopping at his Charger. The mystery of Dani's missing statement would have to wait until tomorrow when the others returned. That didn't settle his mind, though.

Would he get a minute of sleep without his answer?

Chapter Five

Dani had cringed when she got the call from Tyrone about the clean-up for Ingersol, Lynman, and Kash. Since so many days had passed, she thought Kellerman had chosen a different team for the job. But no. They got stuck. At least Tasha was still in the dark about the nearness of the tragedy.

Her roommate sat in the cloth-covered passenger seat chatting away as Dani drove in silence. "Last night, when I started to study for Dr. Zoler's exam, I found that the book I got at the student center was the old edition. The prof specifically called for the new edition, so I'm clueless as to why the bookstore stocked the old one. And this was brand new."

Her roommate took a breath and fingered threads that were unraveling in the door lining. As she laid out the issue with the university bookstore, Dani's mind wandered to a six-foot-two, black-haired man with a smooth, firm jawline and gentle eyes.

She hadn't seen Jay since Friday, but then the sites from the last several days hadn't been initially his. He was bound to stop by today.

Spontaneity wasn't her thing, but maybe she could break her own rules a bit? Go for a spur-of-the-moment walk?

"I was sorta hoping you'd cart me out to the campus at lunch."

"Lunch?" Dani pulled into the parking lot at the marketing firm. Food? Ew. Her stomach felt every morsel of her granola and yogurt from breakfast. She faced the building entrance with unexpected dread as dark clouds reflected in the glassed entrance.

Tasha continued, "By the time I get there for class tonight, the place will be closed. Maybe I can borrow your car?"

Lunch was the last thing she wanted to think about. "No problem. I can take you over there."

Dani shut off the engine. Tasha's phone burst into Walking on Sunshine, and she leaped from the car in her inexhaustible manner. Leaning against the closed door, she twirled one of her blonde curls and talked non-stop.

Dani climbed out slower and eyed the Kellerman van. Tyrone held his phone to his ear but nodded at her. He had to feel the same discomfort she did. Even more since they'd be cleaning through his wife's desk and her personal belongings. She reached back inside for her umbrella and raincoat before locking the doors.

She sauntered toward Tyrone, watching for him to complete his call. He did and swung the door open. "Carla's given me a list of things to bring home to her."

That flung a red flag in her face. "She knows we can't remove anything unless we catalog it for further cleaning at the warehouse or take it to the police."

"I told her that. She calls them odds and ends. A spiral notebook, a flash drive, her coffee mug."

"Why would she want that?" Didn't she have others at home?

"She left her travel mug up here." He grabbed a windbreaker from the seat and shut the door. "I had to tell her I can't. Not while I'm working."

"I bet that wasn't any fun."

"Not nearly as bad as the chewing-out the cop got about taking her phone. The police consider it evidence for some cockamamie reason."

Dani made a face with an animated frown. How could she persuade him to leave her out of the story? "I didn't tell Tasha anything about the murder."

"You're kidding."

She shook her head. "Tasha's been through enough already. We all have." Her roommate had actually bounced back quite well, but her difficulty in January made a good excuse for Dani's request. "Can we, I mean, would it be possible to leave out the fact that this is where Carla works?"

"She's bound to know this is where Carla works. If nothing else, she'll see the photo of us on her desk."

Of course she would. "Then keep the tragedy itself as far away from Tasha as we can." She glanced across the lot at her friend's back. "Don't let her learn that Carla found the body. And even if she does, don't let on that I was with her. As far as she knows, Jay and I had a date."

"Some date." His scowl looked unnatural on his normally smiling face. "I won't lie to her, but I'll try to keep the details under cover. No need to spread gossip. Especially if it will end up terrorizing that poor girl."

Good, he was on board, though Dani hated

misleading him as to her personal agenda.

They geared up and carried their tools toward the entrance where a man in a suit stood with one hand squeezing the other. "Will this take long?"

"I'll be able to give you a better idea once we examine the site." Tyrone opened the glass door and held it for Tasha. She pushed the large dolly, filled with all of their heavy duty machines, into the foyer.

"We've already lost days of work. And there is … such a nightmare still in evidence." He ran his fingers through his thinning, gray hair. The poor man looked like he'd gone without sleep for most of the week. Was he Mr. Ingersol, Mr. Lynman, or Mr. Kash?

"I understand." Tyrone followed Tasha inside.

Dani mustered a smile for the man. "This can't be easy for you, either. Would you like one of us to call when we're almost done?"

He pursed his lips and looked down. "Oh. Oh, I would prefer that. Indeed I would, and yet … It's always been policy that a partner or associate remain on the property anytime the building is open." He shifted his weight to one side. "Yes. Yes, I'll need to stay."

Albert Theisen was an associate. Carla, too. Dani slid her glove off one hand and held it out. "I'm sorry for your loss, Mr. ..."

"Lynman." He shook her hand. "Forgive me, Miss ..."

"Foster."

"Indeed. I'm not exactly myself today. Haven't been sleeping well. No. Not at all really. Not until the office can reopen."

"This type of thing is difficult anyway, but especially if the deceased is a personal friend or coworker."

"Albert was both. Worked with him for years at another agency, so when we opened this one, I begged him to join me." He hesitated. "Join us, that is."

Dani let her gaze wander to the business name

on the door. "So he was a coworker and a friend."

"He was a good man. Smart salesman. Creative contributor. And always positive and enthusiastic."

"Despite his personal trauma."

His eyes narrowed. "I didn't have anything to do with the indiscretion."

Indiscretion? "No, of course not. I didn't mean to insinuate…."

"That story simply leaked out about the missing money, but not from me."

This was getting interesting. She furrowed her eyebrows. "Do you think he embezzled it?"

"Hushhhh." He put his hands up. "No one mentioned embezzling. As far as I know, there isn't any money missing, despite the rumors." He turned away, then back again. "All things can be put to right when we can get back to work."

"Oh, we'll work quickly, Mr. Lynman." She cocked her head. "Still, I can't understand why someone would gossip like that? Slanderous statements about a perfectly good man like Albert

Theisen."

"I never said he was perfect. No. No, not perfect at all. Albert had ambition. Made him an excellent salesman. Put a target on his back though. Arrogant man. Comparable to popular wrestling champions."

"I thought Albert already had quite a bit of money." She didn't want to tip her hand too far.

"Quite a bit of money." His voice became a mumble and he examined his toes. "Quite a bit indeed. That's the problem." He took a few steps away.

Was that it? She'd hoped to drain Mr. Lynman of his information before his weariness took over.

As she lifted her bag, he returned, earnest yet with a sleepy glaze over his eyes. "That's why I had to convince him to come here. He was ready to retire, but I know Albert. I knew him." His gaze drifted right for an instant before returning to her face. "He loved the challenge of creating the perfect promotion. The schmoozing of clients was a game to him. And as nice as he was to most people, he played downright cut-throat when it came to claiming a sale or a contract."

"So he had some enemies." Dani tsked. Totally out of character for her, but she enjoyed role-playing and was learning a lot from Mr. Lynman.

"Not the I'm gonna kill you type of enemies. Only a few I'm not sorry you're gone people. Some who lost out to Albert for the last eight quarters, missing large bonuses, trips, and raises. Yes, he had those types of enemies. Philip Austin hated him all right. So did Steve Nalika and Carla Reid. But jealousy and irritation don't warrant murder."

Dani froze when he mentioned Carla's name. Her friend hadn't hated the man. She'd cried over his death and had nothing but nice things to say about him.

"Well, I'm sure the police will get to the bottom of the issue soon." Pasting on a sympathetic smile, Dani replaced her glove and picked up two large cases filled with tools and supplies. "And don't worry. I have a feeling we'll be done with your clean-up before closing time." Might as well throw the man a fish since he'd shared so much.

He held open the door and followed her into the waiting room. "I don't usually speak out like this … I mean … it's probably the lack of sleep. I shouldn't be saying all this. I hope you'll not … you understand … if you wouldn't mind."

"Oh, don't worry, Mr. Lynman. I'm not a rumor spreader."

Nodding, he raked his hand over his head again and sat on the couch where she and Carla had endured their hours of waiting.

Her stomach soured even more than it had when she forced down her breakfast. Never a good thing when working on the scene of a violent death.

She continued through the doorway. The makeshift hallway had been widened to allow their dolly to come in. Desks, bookshelves and cube walls had already been moved. Tyrone and Tasha struggled with the pieces of the wall that surrounded the crime scene. Dani set her bags beside the water-vac and dragged a section of one wall back the way she came. She left it in the entry.

"What are you doing with that?" Mr. Lynman leaped to his feet.

"We'll be faster if we don't have to maneuver through cube-land. And you want fast, right?" Of course, fast was relative.

Without waiting for his answer, she reentered the office area and used a screwdriver with a head as wide as a dime to unlock another section. Again, she dragged a cumbersome section into the front room. That opened all kinds of space for them to work. Tyrone and Tasha started, but Dani couldn't focus on the cleaning.

Everything was there in front of her exactly as it had been. Only it wasn't the same. Probably things had been moved by Jay or his coworkers. She donned her goggles and mask.

"What's all this?" Tasha stroked her finger across a leather desk chair made almost white by a thin coat of fine powder.

Like the stuff Dani had swatted off her pants. But the chair hadn't been coated when she was there. Even in her agitated state, she would have noticed something like that. Had the cops spilled something on it? But if they had, how had she gotten it on her behind, before they'd arrived?

"I'll take the flat surfaces." Usually one of the last things they did was check the area for errant blood splatter, but since Tyrone was busy pulling up the carpet and Tasha was wiping down every inch of the walls, Dani focused on that weird white stuff.

She glanced at the nearest desk. Albert's, she'd assumed. Looked much like it had before, though the file folders were missing. Maybe they contained evidence?

She stroked a chamois across the surface. Well, none of the powder covering the chair at the other desk had spread over here. No blood splatter either, though she hadn't expected any from the look of the wound.

Hadn't that drawer been open?

Tyrone and Tasha were hard at work and paying no attention. Dani tugged open the drawer, though they didn't normally clean in areas that were closed. The black bottom revealed eraser threads and some dust from a sharpener. None of the white stuff that was in the chair. An unopened roll of TUMS and three plain black pens.

That's what she remembered. An impression fizzed, but she couldn't coax the thought forward. Something was missing from this set up, but for the life of her she had no idea what it was. She pulled out her phone and snapped a picture. Maybe it would come to her later.

"Miss Foster." Frank Durmonde, her stoic boss, stepped through the entrance wearing a medical mask. His orange muffler commanded more attention than his whiny voice. Kellerman's assistant manager had a knack for showing up at the worst possible moments. "Your interest in this location is purely for cleaning purposes. I suggest your photojournalism days are over."

She froze. No. He had no idea what he was talking about. Dani stuffed the phone in her pocket. "Yes, sir." She added a chipper tone that she didn't feel and shoved the drawer closed.

If nothing else, she could ask Jay why the powder was everywhere except the drawer and how the dust had seemed to multiply since she'd first arrived at the crime scene. There had to be some explanation.

Chapter Six

Jay parked outside his latest crime scene, per usual, only this wasn't a usual week. Not since the woman of his interest was also a person of interest in this crime.

He watched through the rain-dotted windshield for the cleaning crew to complete their work inside Ingersol, Lynman, and Kash. Not that he expected them to have found any stray evidence. His team and the detectives had been in and out of the place for days. But talking with Tyrone-and-team had become a debriefing that he needed to put closure on each scene.

And doing it in person allowed him time with Dani during a month when both of them had precious little to spare.

If only they'd had the chance to have a real date before now. One that wasn't set up by their mutual friends. Then, they might have a halfway pleasant memory instead of this disaster to reflect on.

Maybe he should ask her to dinner or coffee? He had some time tonight. Tasha came through the doorway dragging a full dolly. Barely five-foot tall, the blonde threw herself into her task with the fortitude of a bull.

Jay slipped off his sport coat and donned his police jacket to offer a little protection from the thunderstorm that had planted itself overhead. He climbed out of the car and jogged through the downpour to help her out the door. "Everything as expected in there?"

She laughed and flashed him her cheerleader smile. "You worry too much, Officer Hunter."

He tugged the heavy load over the edge of a

metal ramp that spanned the two steps to the surface of the lot. "Maybe."

Tasha angled the dolly toward the white van with Kellerman climbing horizontally across the side while he pushed. "How is it you always know when we'll be finished?" Reaching the van, she unlocked it and lifted the back door.

"I don't. I just come by at the end of my shift. Your scheduler is the one who seems to anticipate how long your jobs will take." He grunted, shoving the dolly up a steeper metal incline attached to the truck's bumper.

"Marla." She tugged the front wheels over the edge of the bed. "You're right. She usually has us done right before lunch or around five pm."

"So I take it y'all didn't find anything unexpected?" He gave one more mighty push to put the rolling platform firmly inside the van.

"Have to talk to Tyrone about that, but nothing I'm aware of."

Good enough for him. Having finished his

task, he left her organizing the cargo area and jogged back toward the building. The large drops pelted him.

Dani shoved a duffel through the entrance from the main room, then turned around and dragged another behind her. Mr. Lynman sat a few feet away paging through a magazine and ignoring her struggle. Jay pushed open the front door. "Can I help you with those?" He reached for the bag she'd hoisted to her shoulder.

Appreciation shone from her lovely eyes. Dressed in skinny jeans and a tee shirt decorated with blue and gray splatters and swirls, she looked nothing if not relieved to be through with this job. And no wonder.

"Thanks so much." She let him take the bag and slipped on the windbreaker she clutched. She pulled the attached hood over her head, shouldered the other bag, and followed him outside.

Distant thunder growled across gray, low-hanging clouds. Jay hurried across the lot and hoisted the heavy burden to the bed of the cargo truck.

"Thanks." Tasha pulled it further into the shelter.

Dani trotted up the ramp. "Come up here and get out of the rain." She carried her bag to the front of the cargo hold.

Jay obeyed. His jacket, water resistant or not, was beginning to soak.

"You two can dry off. I'll be back." Tasha wrapped her bushy hair into a rain cap and darted for the entrance. The blonde corkscrews popped right back out as soon as she made it in the door.

"She's the only girl I know who never has to worry about her hair going flat." Dani chuckled as she slipped the hood off and began securing the machinery and supplies with straps attached to the bed of the hold. "But then, I don't think Tasha worries about much of anything."

"She wasn't concerned about the murder?" Jay slipped his jacket off and gave it a shake near the opening.

"Actually, I didn't tell her about that."

Jay turned his head toward her. How could she have kept something so huge from her best friend?

"After all she went through, the last thing I want is for her to be frightened again."

"I thought you said she doesn't normally worry about things."

Dani bit her bottom lip and avoided his eyes. She set about strapping in a large vacuum. "So when she does get upset, it's really traumatic for her."

Her explanation sounded reasonable, but her attitude seemed off. The missing record of her on the reports drifted across his memory. With his captain gone all weekend, he'd not had the chance to iron out that little detail. "About that …."

Her gaze moved to the doorway. "Oh, hold on. I'll be back." She yanked her hood back on, ducked her head and darted into what had lessened to a heavy sprinkle. Tyrone shoved a huge cart full of bags and tools out of the door. Tasha guided it to the ramp, and Dani joined her to brace the load on the slight incline from the building. With Dani and Tyrone pushing, Tasha ran ahead onto the ramp and into the truck. Jay joined her at the edge of the ramp as the load reached it. He tugged on the edge while stabilizing a top-heavy load. Between the four of them, they finally shoved the cargo onto the truck. Tasha and Dani secured it while Jay and Tyrone retrieved the two ramps.

"Thanks for the assistance. Another set of muscles is always welcome." Ty shot him a broad smile.

"Things good inside?" Jay carried one side of the smaller slopes to the truck.

"Good enough." Tyrone tilted his head. "Not so much with my wife."

"She's still upset?"

"One of your detective friends gave her the don't leave town speech. Like she could have anything to do with that man's death."

Jay had been afraid the suspicion would turn her direction because of what Dr. Konn had said. "Don't let it get to her. I know she didn't have anything to do with it, but a person at the scene, covered in blood and found alone with the body, is always going to be a suspect. It's not personal." They shoved the first incline onto the bed and moved to slide the longer metal ramp into the base of the truck bed.

"Personal to me. To her, too." Tyrone slammed down the latch that held the metal in place.

Jay put a hand on his friend's shoulder. "I'll do what I can, but I think this will go away on its own as the detectives learn more."

"What if it doesn't?" He faced him, forcing him to drop his hand. "What if one of those guys decides she's the best bet and works to make the evidence back him up?"

Not that such things didn't happen, but only with good reason. "It's too early to tell which direction this will go, but I can't imagine suspicion for Carla lasting. They might already have moved onto someone else."

Tyrone's jaw worked.

"It's gonna be okay, man." Jay smacked his friend's thick bicep. "You'll see."

He offered a short nod.

"What's up with you, big guy?" Tasha moved to the edge of the truck with Dani in her tracks. "I'd have thought you'd be laughing at our drenched selves. Did you even catch a droplet?"

"Not so much." He reached up to catch her as she jumped down.

Jay eyed Dani and lifted his hands. She turned her back and used the two-rung ladder on the corner, pulling the cord that lowered the door as she came. "Thanks anyway." Slipping off her windbreaker, she tugged her tight knot of hair apart. Chocolate waves bounced against her shoulders, and she combed her fingers through her bangs.

Tyrone shot the bolt and latched a heavy-duty lock onto the gate before he strode to the front of the van.

Jay started to encourage him more but found Dani walking away. "Hey, wait a minute."

Tasha had fallen into step beside her, and both halted and turned making a scraping sound on the wet concrete.

"I … well." He lifted his hand toward Dani and glanced at Tasha. Take the hint. Not that he wouldn't politely shoo her away like a pesky fly, but he'd rather send the message without being a jerk about it.

Dani handed the blonde her keys. "I'll be right there." She closed the gap between them. "You wanted something?"

What? Coffee? Dinner? "I thought you might like to see what I finished from last night." What was he thinking? He couldn't waltz her into the station to see items from an ongoing investigation. Then again, she had been a witness, so he had a good excuse.

"You mean with that laser thingy you were

using?"

Her interest was piqued. And why not? The latest-greatest technology to come down the pipe was likely to intrigue anyone.

"I can take you home afterward." This wasn't the first date he wanted, but if nothing else, it would give him a chance to find out why her name was missing from the report.

Chapter Seven

Sitting in the smooth, leather-like upholstery of Jay's car threatened to lull Dani's senses. But she couldn't relax, couldn't let him get too close. Her walls needed to stay in place, as much for his safety as for her own. She tugged at a string on the knee of her jeans, making a tiny hole appear.

Jay settled next to her, the black console separating them. After pulling from the lot in silence, he let his hand dangle on top of the gear shift. "So everything was as expected inside?"

Thank you God, that he only wants to talk about the scene. Please keep my secrets safe. She could focus on the job. "Not exactly."

He jerked his head toward her.

"Not that you missed anything." Boy, she could have done that better.

His shoulders relaxed. "You were there. What wasn't right?"

She pictured the scene, what she could remember of it. Maybe her memory was the biggest issue. "I might be recalling it wrong."

The line between his eyebrows deepened. "It's not often that you see the scene before and after. But remember, we tend to move things as we're working. Measuring, photographs, fingerprints."

"That's probably what happened." Though none of that explained the powder-covered chair.

He flashed a half-smile. "I have a feeling you're gonna love this new piece of technology. It perfects my memory." He went on to explain some of the details of the digital reconstruction from the laser scan. Most of it went over Dani's head, but she enjoyed Jay's enthusiasm. He practically lit up.

"Wow. You've really found your niche, Jay Hunter."

"What makes you say that?"

"You get so excited about your job. It's obvious that you truly love it. And you don't have to tell me that you're one of the best at what you do. The other cleaning teams always complain about the evidence they have to submit because it's been missed. But you and your team rarely miss anything."

He chuckled. "I don't know about that." Was he blushing under all that tan? His lips pressed together, and he wiped them with his hand before hanging it across the shifter knob again. "How 'bout we do that date thing after visiting the station. Maybe dinner?"

She glanced at the hole in her knee, barely noticeable, but she knew it was there. And her hair needed to be washed from the sweat of wearing the helmet all day. Though they had planned an after-work day before, she'd prepared for it. Extra clothes, makeup bag. Today, not so much. And while spontaneity worked for Tasha, it wasn't her favorite trait. "Um … maybe another time?"

"Okay." He nodded, but the spark she'd seen evaporated as he pulled into the lot and parked in a numbered space. He climbed out and strolled around the car.

She started to get out on her own. She was at the police station, for pity's sake. But he was a gentleman. She found that out during their crazy escapade back in January. Didn't seem to matter if the lady was a date, friend, or perfect stranger, he always held doors. He opened it wide now and offered his hand. She didn't hesitate like she'd done before. But unlike then, he dropped her hand as soon as she stood.

She'd noticed the same thing when he took her to her apartment the other night. Though he'd been more than kind. Rather romantic. Even if he hadn't held her hand like he did after the accident in January.

Maybe she was imagining her hand as a hot potato, but his release of it left it dangling with nothing to do and no place to be. She smoothed her jeans and shouldered her purse, but her hand still felt bare and awkward. Finally, she clasped them both behind her and fell into step next to Jay as they crossed the cement.

Rows of naked trees separating the car lines showed signs of buds. Looked promising. After February leveled a cold, clammy claw over the whole state, she was ready for some springtime.

She followed him through a side door where he'd swiped his security card. "Photo ID?"

"Naturally, security is an issue." He stepped to a desk and filled out some type of form. Probably her name on a visitor's list. Great. Another record of her being here.

She eyed the security badge clipped to his lapel. "Can I see it?" Did he photograph as good as he looked?

He held it out then engaged an officer that

approached the desk from the other side. Dani scanned the image. Not bad, though his smile was more charming than the all-business grimace showing on the card. Maybe mean was the posture he'd tried to present?

He slipped a lanyard around her neck. "Do I pass inspection?"

She handed the tag back and looked up at him. "Somehow, I think you could take a better picture than that." The firm, clean-shaved jaw, his sensitive dark eyes, muscular shoulders, trim waistline. He would certainly be fun to photograph. Especially if he used that intriguing half-smile that he showed when he was about to say something funny.

He stared at it a second. "I never paid much attention. As long as it looked like me, that's all that mattered."

"A picture can have the same features as the subject without really looking like them. This one doesn't represent you well at all."

"You sound like a photographer." He smiled

and led her down a hallway.

Her face heated. Not for a long time. One of the many things she'd had to shed from her life.

Jay paused at an office, and she almost bumped into him. He knocked on the open door. "Captain, I want to show off the 3D laser scanner."

"Thought you'd gone home, Hunter."

"I left all right, but I can't get enough of this place." He chuckled and displayed the half-grin.

Her heart sped.

"I've got one of the witnesses from Ingersol here. Wanted to share the data I pulled. To refresh her memory." He held out his hand toward her. "I think you interviewed Miss Foster."

Late into the night as a matter of fact. Dani joined Jay in the entryway. The other man's mouth flattened. Never a good sign, but then he'd probably hoped never to lay eyes on her again after all of the complications she brought into the mix.

And technically, she was no longer a witness, not that Jay realized that. Would the captain deny the request and have to explain, or would he avoid the conflict to keep from revealing too much about her?

"Go ahead." Eerie how the man's mouth moved without any semblance of emotion or animation. No nod or shrug. Almost like a mannequin.

"Thanks." Jay didn't seem to notice anything weird about the exchange. Good.

He took her to another room, darkened with panels on the wall. "I don't get to work in here very often, but I enjoyed the experience these last few days." He paused at a laptop computer that scanned his thumbprint.

"What's here?"

He tapped for a moment. "This." The panels lit with images of the cube at Ingersol, Lynman, and Kash. Each of the four panels contained a full-sized photo of the wall of the cubicle, as well as the floor and ceiling to about six feet from the wall.

She faced the panel that held an image of the

opening and Albert's desk and chair. They had to be his since the other wall had Ty's picture. The dead man's face showed. Creepy, but thorough. She scanned the image, stopping at the desk. "That." She pointed. "That was different. That desk drawer was open when I was there."

He sat down at the computer for a moment and the images disappeared. "We took one-foot scans all the way to the ceiling. Every one of them shows that desk drawer shut." He reinstated the panels she'd been viewing. "What makes you think it was open?"

"When I saw the guy … deceased … Albert Theisen, I wanted to get something to stop the bleeding. Anything. I knew I couldn't leave fingerprints, but that drawer was open. I thought about it today while I was cleaning. It had some black pens and a package of TUMS. And maybe something else." She scrapped her thumbnail across her lip. "I can't remember, but I do remember the pens and TUMS. They were still there today."

"That's odd. Maybe Carla shoved closed when she left. Not thinking about it?"

Not likely, but not worthy of a debate. Dani turned to the left where the complete body of the man lay at the edge of the wall. Part of a puddle of blood had seeped onto the carpet from the stab wounds in his chest. She turned to the back wall. The chair for the second desk was covered with white dust, the way it had been when they had arrived that morning to clean. "That was something else out of place."

"The chair?" He tilted his head. "It probably got moved when the doc came in to do his preliminary exam."

"No. I mean, yes, it was moved, but it wasn't covered with dust like that."

He rubbed his chin. "I don't remember wiping it down, but someone else could have."

"I'm not saying this well at all. There wasn't any dust on it when we first found the body. There wasn't dust anywhere." Well, except on the floor where she fell. But that had been at the entrance. Probably more than six feet away.

"What do you see?" Jay came up behind her.

Though he didn't touch her, his warmth radiated to her back. She swallowed and forced her mind to remain on track. "You can't see it. But I … sort of … sat there inside the doorway. And then I had this layer of dust that looked like the stuff in the chair all over my backside." Carla had mentioned face powder, but it was whiter and finer, like dust. "It might not have been the same thing, but I can't imagine where else it could have come from."

He turned away from her and advanced to the back wall photo. "If that's true, then all of this area would have been covered with the dust, and it wasn't."

"Except that the chair was clean when Carla and I were there and was full of white stuff when you got there."

His eyes shot to hers and his mouth opened

then shut. His gaze wandered toward the floor, and he began to pace to his right. "So it wasn't. Then it was."

Was he making sense? "Almost sounds like you're studying the biblical account of creation."

He chuckled. "I guess it could." He pulled a bright red coffee cup from a drawer. "Say this mug isn't here." He set it on the computer desk. "Then it is. There are a number of ways that mug could now be there."

A number of ways? "You can put it there … like you did."

"Yes … and?"

She stared at the mug. "Someone else could put it there."

"True … any other way?"

She pursed her lips and shifted them to her right. "Well, if it fell there, it would have broken, or at the very least not be upright."

He put a Kleenex box in front of the mug. "What if it was always there but hidden?"

"Camouflaged."

"Exactly. Was there anything on the chair that would have kept you from seeing the dust?" He advanced to an actual chair next to the picture and turned it around. "Maybe it was facing away from you?"

She shut her eyes and concentrated. She had reached the cube entrance and focused on Carla. But there was the chair, facing her like someone had recently gotten up from it. And nothing was in it. No sweater, no jacket. Nothing.

She shook her head. "I'm sure it was facing me, nothing in it at all. Including dust. I would have noticed that. I saw it right away this morning."

"So how'd it get there?"

Same question. Hadn't they exhausted the possibilities? She stared at the red mug. "Wait. We're not talking about a piece of porcelain."

"That was just an example."

"Yes, but the mug would break. Dust falls. It always falls and it's light enough to spread over a large space."

"Then why wasn't there dust on the body?"

"Because the body was here." Dani spun to the right side of the cube. "While the chair was all the way over here." She crossed to the corner leaving a little room for the desk against the wall. "Of course the cube was smaller than this room, but it's still easy to see why this area could be covered and this one left alone."

"Yet it fails to explain how dust fell there …" He pointed to where she stood. "… and at the entrance but didn't hit the man that lay between the two areas."

She didn't like the conjecture that her brain was brewing. "Do you know what the powder was?"

"Still in analysis."

"You think it might have been from the ceiling tiles?" She turned toward him as he faced the entrance.

His chin went up. "I suppose, though I can't

imagine why. Maybe the killer climbed over the cubicle wall to catch Theisen by surprise?"

Possible. "But what if …." She put her hand on his forearm, then paused, totally losing her train of thought. "Wow, you do weights, huh?" She squeezed her eyes shut. "Did I say that out loud?"

Jay laughed outright, looking down at her. "Yeah." He chuckled again. "Thanks."

"Forget I said that. Sometimes my mouth works without my mind attached."

"I've noticed. It's okay."

She released him. "Look that way." She fanned her face when he turned away from her. Good thing the room was only partly lit. "See the tile directly above the chair?" She pointed out the mottled square. "See how it isn't entirely even with the others?"

He stepped closer to the panel. "You mean where that corner is raised?"

"Exactly."

"Not all folks are like you, Dani. For most

people, close is good enough."

"You see any other tiles that are good enough?" She walked a smooth circle.

He scanned each wall. "I can set up those measurements to be sure, but it looks like the others are the same level." He turned to face her in the center of the room. "So you think someone came through the ceiling?"

She nodded.

"That still doesn't explain why the dust wasn't on the chair, then all of a sudden was." He pointed at the whitened chair.

"Unless the murderer waited until Carla and I left then went back into the ceiling before you came." Not a fun prospect.

His eyes widened. "You think he was there? When you and Carla found the body, he was still in the building?"

"Gruesome thought, but yes. I think he was there the entire time you all analyzed the scene. Somewhere up in the ceiling, waiting for the chance to leave without a trace."

"So the dust at the entrance was where he came down?"

"He drops down, kills Albert, then hears us and hides around the corner. When we leave, he goes back up in the ceiling."

His eyebrows lowered. "Why come back, though? Why this cube?"

She shrugged. Good question. "Maybe he left something behind?"

He put his hand at the small of her back. "I better get you home."

A tingle exploded in her senses at his touch.

The captain came to his door as they neared it. "Thought I heard you, Hunter."

"Yes, Sir? Something you need?"

"Durwood and Perriman brought in the Ingersol killer. The guy's ex-wife. She's not confessed, but close." He shut a file folder and turned back toward his desk. "Guess you don't have to worry about bringing in witnesses anymore."

So much for all the details she and Jay had figured out.

Jay's eyes narrowed. "Thanks for letting me know." He turned his inquisitive gaze toward Dani for a second, then resumed his stroll toward the exit. "Something's not right."

"Why? Because a woman killed the guy?" Surely he wasn't being narrow-minded like that.

He snorted. Reaching the desk, he signed her out on the book. She returned the lanyard, and they emerged into the dwindling sunlight. "I'll go through the report again. Maybe it will hit me."

Uh-oh. The last thing she needed was for him to go back through the report. "Isn't the case closed?"

"I'll still look at it. There are some things that don't click."

Time for a diversion. "If nothing else, this will make Tyrone and Carla feel better."

"Yeah, there's that." He smoothed his hand along the side of his head. "Ty's been bugging the tar out of me over the fact that she's been a suspect. Like I wouldn't change that if I could."

Good thing Tyrone might be back to his natural good mood tomorrow, but, other than that, the news of this woman's arrest felt all wrong.

Chapter Eight

Jay pulled out his phone for the umpteenth time and rested his elbows on his Formica desktop. Despite the calamity of their almost-date last week, he needed to try again with Dani. A planned-ahead night out. Not something cooked up by his buds or a spur-of-the moment invitation.

She had practically glowed the other night as she pointed out the different things in the scene panels. A smile tickled the corner of his mouth. Though the announcement of Mrs. Theisen's arrest seemed to make her enthusiasm wane, it hadn't squelched his.

A rumble of a conversation grew. One of the other guys on his team wove through the desks talking basketball with a detective … Perriman. Just the man he'd wanted to speak to.

He pocketed his phone and joined Perriman in the aisle. "Did you get a confession yet?" Winnie Theisen had proved a stouter wall than first expected.

The detective slowed. "Not yet. She lied about her alibi at first. That put up flags, but I'm not sure we'll have enough for a conviction."

Jay fell into step beside him, struggling for the words that wouldn't invite further suspicion for Carla. "How about her boyfriend?"

Perriman lifted his gaze to the ceiling. "Darren Balducci. That guy's a piece of work. He was down in Austin at a self-actualization conference. Something to convince him that he has potential." He laughed.

"Checked it out?" Of course they had, but the whole thing felt backward.

"Flights, hotel registration. He even ordered a huge meal about two in the afternoon and enough adult movies to last him all night long."

Jay followed him toward the break room. "K. So what else? She has a motive—Albert's money."

"Which she gets none of if she's convicted." Perriman rubbed his thumb and forefinger together. "But those odds are getting worse by the moment. She has no alibi, but we can't place her at the scene or put a weapon into her hand."

"Perriman." Durwood came around the corner and stopped the man short.

"See you, Hunter." He about-faced, meeting his partner at the hallway and disappearing around the corner.

His exit left Jay eyeing a Diet Pepsi in the machine and mulling over their conversation. The pieces of the puzzle felt forced. He turned away from the machine and strolled toward the lab. In fact, everything about Theisen's murder and the investigation left an odd taste.

He slowed as he came upon Captain Madison's office. There was one thing he could try to get cleared up. He tapped on the wood of the partially opened door.

"Come." The man's deep baritone rang out. He sounded relaxed if not pleasant.

"Do you have a minute, Sir?"

"Hunter? Sure. What do you need?" He looked up from his seat at his desk, his pen poised above a clipboard.

Jay balanced his hand on the knob and took a step inside the office. "Answers. Well, one answer. Why was Dani Foster's name removed from the witness record?"

The captain didn't move.

"The woman you interviewed after the Theisen murder."

A blank expression met Jay. Not a curious or confused one, but a flat cartoon.

"Here in your office. I was outside when you finished." And he wasn't going to let the matter drop.

Captain Madison lowered his hand and began writing on the paper in front of him as though Jay had evaporated.

"I've never known you to eliminate a witness."

The man continued to write at his desk as the silence grew. Finally, he paused. His gaze crawled up to Jay, though his head remained perfectly still as he regarded him over the rims of his glasses.

Jay released the door and widened his stance to a comfortable shoulder width distance. Prepared to wait out this stare-down, he clasped his hands in front of him and met the captain's look.

Putting down the pen, Madison sighed. "I feared removing her name would cause undue attention. Didn't expect it to come from you."

"Why was it removed?"

"By request. From someone with more clout than you and me put together." He picked up his pen again. "And that's all I have to say about it, so you might as well go on."

Jay grimaced. Clout. Who did Dani know? He returned to the corner he shared with Cal, but the detail gnawed at him.

Pulling out his phone, he found Dani's contact info and hit the link. Now he had an even better reason for asking her for a date. After all, what was the worst that could happen?

For a moment, he couldn't decide if a no or a yes would be the better answer.

As the phone rang, he scanned the data coming in on his computer screen. Slow days were always hard. Not that he wanted a new homicide to pop up. But after being so busy all month, a backlog of random paperwork and data scans threatened to overwhelm him.

Another reason he wanted to be a detective. Their slow days consisted of examining cold cases—re-analyzing details and stirring up new possibilities.

Dani picked up on the third ring. "Is this Jay or Officer Hunter?"

"Which would you prefer?" He couldn't let that dangling worm go by without at least a nibble.

"Definitely prefer Jay, since Officer Hunter would likely be calling with difficult questions for me to answer."

"I'd say that's probably a good choice. Are you busy tomorrow night?" Rip that Band-Aid right off. He picked up his pen, twirling and tapping it to the ever-present rhythm in his head. A holdover from high school drum line.

"Um … no." She drew out the word. "What did you have in mind?"

"Nothing extravagant. There's a movie downtown. Outdoors. Thought it might be fun."

"I didn't know there were drive-ins here."

"Not a drive-in. I mean, there are some around, I think, but this is more like a park."

"Downtown?" She paused. "Downtown Dallas?"

He smiled. She was interested, in the movie at least. Not that he was into romantic comedies, but this Sandra Bullock one had become a classic. "Yes. I can't really describe it. You'll have to see it for yourself."

"Hmm. Tempting. Okay, what can I bring?"

Unanticipated question. "Well, I've got lawn chairs and a blanket. What would you like to have on hand to drink?"

"Why don't you let me take care of drinks and snacks? You like unsweet tea, right?"

Sounded like she was already warming up to the idea. He ironed out the details and ended the call. That went better than expected. Maybe he'd get a simple answer to his question.

And he hoped he could piece together a few hours alone with her before he got called away again.

Jay had told her not to do anything elaborate. He didn't say she couldn't cook. That thought consoled Dani as she unpacked her large tote full of lettuce wraps, kettle corn, and chocolate chip cookies. At least she'd changed her mind about the spinach and artichoke heart dip. Overkill, and there wouldn't have been a place to keep it warm anyway.

"Wow, some spread." Jay laid a metal tray on a short, canvas camping table, or maybe it was a stool?

She added her plastic storage containers and opened their lids. "I never knew this was a park up here."

He unfolded a lawn recliner. "It's only been up here a few years. There used to be several small bridges crossing the freeway. And they weren't all necessary for the new flow of downtown traffic. So the city filled in the space between them and designed an urban playground."

"It's beautiful. I've driven under it several times." She scooped up a cup full of ice from the small insulated carrier she'd brought and filled it with tea for Jay.

"I hope you like romantic comedy." He took the cup and sat.

Ugh. Is that what they were seeing? Some icky-sweet love story with a perfect happily ever after? Like that ever resembled real life. Please, Lord, don't let it have a dog in it. She poured a glass for herself and took a sip. "Umm." Let him figure out if she was toasting the tea or the movie.

"They tend to show the older ones up here—Must Love Dogs, Marley and Me."

This was going to have a dog in it, wasn't it?

"Either that, or they show recorded stage versions of operas that have performed all over the world."

Opera? Kill me now. Her dad's words floated through her mind, but she stifled the smile. Her old man had gone to his first opera kicking and screaming but found he actually enjoyed it. Even bought tickets for Dani and him for the next show. "Do you like opera?"

He shrugged. "I like a place to relax. If I enjoy what's showing, I stay. If I don't like the show, I pack up my chair or blanket and walk a bit. Downtown has a unique feel that you can't find in the rest of the city and certainly not in the suburbs."

"Like a pulse. A drum beat. I know what you mean." And a totally different environment from her neighborhood. The apartment complex and streets of houses that surrounded it had little sound at all besides an occasional eighteen-wheeler on the nearby freeway.

Here, the traffic changed the tone of the background noise constantly, as vehicles of different sizes whirred around them. The building lights displayed apartment living at its most stylish and an abundance of offices.

Like the one where Albert had been killed. While Jay filled a plastic plate, Dani wrapped up in the navy and yellow letterman sweater that Tasha had bought for her at a second hand store.

"All these buildings remind me of Carla's

office."

"Except hers is a one-story."

True. "You ever noticed how offices tend to look alike?"

After biting into a lettuce wrap, he paused a moment before answering. "Is there a right or wrong answer here?"

She giggled.

He drank from his water bottle and replaced the cap. "They should. They're basic empty rooms with wall- and floor-jacks. Companies move in and set up the configuration of their choice."

"But they all have similar ceilings." She pointed to the building closest to them where the tile grid looked exactly like Carla's. "People don't usually notice them."

"Except you, when they aren't even." He chuckled, his dark eyes highlighted by the glow of a building somewhere behind her, caused her to lose her breath for a moment.

Tearing her gaze away, she nodded, willing her

heart to slow down.

"You're thinking back to your hypothesis." He leaned forward and collected a cookie from the tray. "It was really a brilliant idea, you know?"

Brilliant? Her? Did he really mean that? The lights along the sidewalk dimmed, and the movie began. She recognized the introduction to While You Were Sleeping right away. Her stomach clinched. Not this movie. Sandra Bullock's character had a background way too close to her own. Could she force herself to sit through this film?

Jay's phone played The Ants Go Marching. He glanced at the screen. "Uh oh. Excuse me." He stood and picked his way through movie watchers toward a bank of trees. "Yes, sir."

The brief reply was all Dani heard, but enough to realize their date was over. Could a half-hour drive and ten-minute conversation be counted as an official date? If so, this made two. That is, if the trip to the station the other night was number one. Hard to tell.

If nothing else, Jay Hunter kept her guessing. She replaced the lids to the food and packed it away in her bag. She had the stool and one of the chairs folded by the time he returned.

Silently, he folded the other chair and collected all the furniture. She followed him out, dragging a mini ice chest on wheels behind her. They reached the arched walkway. "That was the captain. There's been another murder not far from here."

He was in Special Investigator mode. Funny how she could tell the difference in his off-duty and on-duty attitudes. Even more interesting that she liked him either way.

"I'll have to take you there, but I'll find someone to transport you home right away."

"I don't mind staying. Maybe I'll see something interesting."

He glanced at her but didn't smile.

Probably not the right thing to say. "I don't mean that you'll miss something, but I am pretty observant."

"Yes, you are." He looked at her again. His eyes softened, and he slowed as he reached his car and popped the trunk. "I'm not intimidated by your observation skills, Dani. This is a crime scene, though. Someone committed a murder. The height of evil, desperation, and recklessness."

After they deposited all of the cargo in his trunk, he turned toward her and rubbed a hand along her forearm. "I don't want to see you in danger. Not again."

Even through her sweater sleeve, the pressure of his hand on her arm warmed her. "I'm not, and I won't be, even on the site. Which I'll probably be cleaning anyway come Monday."

"Likely." He turned and laid his hand at the small of her back as he guided her around the car. "But whoever killed the person at the scene might still be about."

"You're thinking of the fact that Albert's murderer was probably still on site when Carla and

I found his body."

"Seems likely to me. You were at risk and didn't realize it. Isn't that the way things often work? It's the spider hiding in your shoe that causes the problems."

Spider? Ick. "Oh, thanks for the image. I'm going to have nightmares about putting on my sneakers, now."

He laughed.

She stopped at the passenger door and let him open it. "But seriously, surrounded by police isn't a dangerous place to be, as far as I'm concerned." Though staying alone with him for much longer would slow her ability to think clearly.

He seated himself before he commented. "It's a moot point anyway. I don't have time to take you home and come back. It's not like this hasn't happened before."

Really? He often took his dates to crime scenes? She leveled a stare at him.

He glanced her direction. "I don't mean it's

happened to me before." He refocused out the windshield. "But even the lieutenant had to bring his wife to a hotel where a suicide took place. He couldn't very well drop her along the roadside. That's why we have round-the-clock shifts."

"And yet, they're still calling you in from off-duty?"

"Criminals don't always cooperate with our schedule. I'm on call. Always. That's why it's so hard to carry on relationships. Even friendships."

Her job felt the same way sometimes, though they didn't often get called out late-night. "So you're part of the second string?" She smirked. That title wouldn't go over very well, but she couldn't resist the tease.

"More like third or fourth after the last several weeks. Though all of us have been twenty-four/seven for a while." He took an exit. "You'll need to stay in the car until I say to get out."

Anticipation churned an excited, queasy feeling she remembered from her adolescence. "At this point, you could tell me to lie under the car, and I'd be okay. I remember when my dad used to bring home case files to look through. We'd puzzle through things for hours." She'd even helped him solve a crime one time when she noticed a tiny detail in the photographs that he hadn't seen.

"Your dad was a cop? A detective?"

Oh, no. Had she really told him that? She stared at the lights along the freeway. "Have I never mentioned that?"

"No. Where did he work?"

His voice showed nothing but natural interest. Not pushy. A good guy who only wanted to get to know her better. "A little town … north of here." Technically she hadn't lied. It was further north. And a little smaller than Dallas.

He broke into a story about a crime occurring in the rural area of East Texas where he grew up. "I was amazed that the chief was able to glean so much information off of a piece of an ice cream wrapper." He glanced at her. "I guess that was probably my first taste of police work. After that I couldn't get enough of it."

He parked in front of the single-story building that looked very much like Ingersol, Lynman, and Kash.

She gasped. "This place looks like Carla's office."

"It's a business building. They look alike." He smiled and shut off the car. "Remember?"

"But you have to see the similarities between these crime scenes."

"We're not even inside, yet. Strike that. I'm not inside. You're staying out here." He opened his car door. "Besides, this is more a school than a business. A tutoring place for at-risk kids."

She watched him load up with gear and head toward the building.

Judith Albright Center for Alternative Education. Hmm. Maybe he was right. But the tingling at the back of her head convinced her to keep her eyes open.

Chapter Nine

The place, a low, dark-brick building, did bear a striking resemblance to the offices for Carla's marketing company. But Albert Theisen's murderer, his ex-wife, was in jail. The killings couldn't be connected.

He glanced back and shot a smile in Dani's direction before entering the building. This one didn't have as much glass as the last one—the wall came to about waist-high—but the reception area, the couches, even the bathrooms, indicated the same plan. Maybe even the same builder.

He maneuvered through the opening behind

another marble counter. As expected, a large room. This one was filled with bare tables instead of cubes. Two chairs were tucked under each one on opposite corners. All except on the far side of the room where a table with a collapsed leg lay on its side near the body of a man.

Jay eyed the area. Most particularly, the broken tile that hung from the metal grid in the ceiling. He set his bags down, eyed Cal who stood near the body, and pointed upward.

Cal nodded and extended a mounted mirror a few feet. As he inched it through the gaping hole, Jay set down his bags and yanked his gun from his holster. He watched his partner's face. The chances of anyone hiding up there, after the obvious arrival of police, were tiny, but criminals had been known to be stupid.

After a few moments, Cal shook his head. "Empty." He retracted the extension and pulled a toothpick from his mouth, gesturing with it. "I look forward to seeing the scan, though." He clamped down on it again. Two other specialists from his team came through the entrance along with a uniformed officer.

Jay began to unpack his tools, making mental notes of the scene. The victim, a male in his mid to late-sixties, lay face down at the edge of the broken furniture. One chair had toppled backwards.

"Not a lot of blood." Cal pulled his toothpick from his mouth again and tucked it into his shirt pocket. "No wounds on his back." He donned a pair of latex gloves.

Jay followed suit. "How did the table break?" The man seemed to have fallen next to it, his legs extended. "If he fell on it, he'd either still be there, or be crumpled, bent-legged, like he'd slid off as it broke."

"So he didn't break it?" Cal raised one eyebrow. "Someone fell from the ceiling and broke it?"

"Quite a fall." Jay eyed the distance. "Certain injury, a sprain or a break … unless the person dropped from up there on purpose."

"Crashed the table, which alerted this guy."

"Robbery gone wrong?" Seemed plausible. "But he couldn't get back up that way." He raised his finger. "Because of the broken table. How or where did he go?"

They scanned the ceiling. Dani's sharp eyes would have helped at this point, but her presence would break protocol, not to mention Jay's concentration. He was already distracted by her even though she sat outside.

He gave an internal growl and refocused on his surroundings. A few tiles over the grid bar displayed an uneven edge. "There?" He eyed the table beneath the area. White dust, not nearly so much as at Carla's office, but enough. "Same dust as at the Ingersol office."

"What's your plan, kid?" Cal unlatched the case with the laser scanner.

"Me? Isn't Gates coming?"

Lieutenant Gates, their supervisor, usually

coordinated the team before leaving them to do their jobs.

"Huh-uh. He's outta town. Told me to handle things, but I see that look in your eye. You're already half-way to figuring this thing out, aren't you?"

Only if a jailed person could commit murder. Unless the one in jail didn't kill Albert Theisen in the first place. "Okay. I want a scan of the room from three sides." He pointed out the locations. "And a central scan from there, as well as one of the crawlspace through the broken tile."

"You got it." Cal began to set up the scanner.

"I want the interior beams dusted in the crawl space, at the broken tile and on this one." He pointed above his head. "Who found the body?"

The uniformed cop, Ruidosa, raised a finger at Jay on his return trip to the reception area. He explained how the custodian had found her boss when she came to clean up. "The victim is Ralph Canzonari, the maintenance manager. Divorced, no kids, and about to retire in a few months."

Ruidosa introduced Jay to the stricken Hispanic woman. Tears had reddened her eyes. She held out a shaking hand, which he took in a gentle grip as he greeted her in his limited Spanish.

She poured out her story. He had to stop her a few times to query about vocabulary words, but figured out her statement without Ruidosa's help.

Thank the Lord for regular mission trips to Mexico. Between them and some of his best friends' parents, he'd become fairly fluent throughout high school and college.

Concluding his conversation, he glanced up. Dani sat out in the parking lot, probably bored to death. He still couldn't take her home. And everyone on the scene was working. But at least he could check on her. He stepped into the darkness and jogged toward the car.

She opened the door as he arrived and stuck out one leg. "Can I come in, now?"

Whoa. Not his plan. Especially not on this, his

first case to lead. "I think someone should get a break soon and be able to take you home."

She tilted her head, and her shoulders slumped. "I can take a bus home." She held out her hand as a lighted DART transport rumbled to a stop at the covered bench on the other side of the lot.

He glanced into the illuminated building. "You really want to go in there?"

"At least let me use the facilities."

That wouldn't be a problem. She wouldn't be anywhere near the scene of the crime if all she did was visit the restroom. "All right. But stay in the waiting room. After all, you said yourself that y'all will probably have the scene in a day or two. And you likely will." He put his hand to her back and strolled toward the entrance.

"I know." She smiled at him. "But it would be fun to watch you work."

Why did he suddenly feel like a strutting peacock? How juvenile. How ridiculous. He held the door open for her. "We'll see. For now, wait out here." Struggling to keep his thoughts on the scene, he went through the entrance and down a short hallway to the main room of the building.

Cal carried the scanner to another part of the room. "Your girl still all right out there?"

"She's in the reception area." Wait, so was his witness. "Holt." He motioned to a female officer. "Please take Mrs. Vega to the station to finalize her statement there."

"You shoulda had her take your girl home." Cal finished positioning the camera.

"Dani's not going to get into trouble."

"Look, things like this happen when people get called in from off-duty." He set the timer while Jay retreated several steps down a hallway toward the back of the building. Cal joined him as the machine whirred into action. "Remember when the lieutenant had to bring his wife?"

"On their way home from church."

Cal laughed, then sobered. "But you're not the lieutenant." So much for Cal relieving a difficult situation. "Make sure she stays out there."

From his lips to God's ears.

Wiping her hands on a paper towel, Dani emerged from the ladies room and looked for the woman who had been sitting on the couch. If her own interrogation had been any indication, she'd be able to overhear all of the juicy details. If she could find the lady. She neared the glass and put her hand up to cut the glare. Sure enough, the woman was climbing into a police cruiser. So much for that idea.

At least Dani wasn't the one getting stuck in the back of a cop's car.

After thumbing through a magazine, she wandered to the entrance of the main room. A wall blocked her view of most of the wide area. She could hear the policemen in discussion but couldn't ascertain their words.

Venturing a little further inside, hands clasped in front so she wouldn't accidentally touch something, she caught a glimpse of Jay. Not the tallest man in the room, but almost. He was standing beside a table. Someone stood on top of the table—only his body to his armpits showed, as the rest of him was lost in a hole in the ceiling. And Jay was pointing to a section of broken tile near the corner of the room.

That confirmed it. There was a connection to these two murders.

Officer Cutter rounded the corner and halted as Dani jumped. He slipped his gloves off and stuck them in his blue jean pocket. "Honey, you're gonna get both of you into hot water." He glanced back at the rest of the team, showing Dani a balding spot on the back of his head. For all of his dark hair and young clothes style, the guy had to be almost fifty.

"I didn't touch anything, only wanted to watch you all." She sounded like such a child, even to her own ears.

He took her arm and aimed her out the doorway. "If someone else were to see you standing there, you'd get the third degree, and your fellow in there would lose the respect he's currently building."

"You're his partner, right?" She didn't remember when she learned that, but she was sure of her fact. "Cutter?"

He nodded and nudged her toward the couch. "Call me Cal." He fished a toothpick from his shirt pocket and tucked it between his teeth. "You got someone who can pick you up?"

Really? Couldn't she even talk to Jay? "I thought I could wait here?"

"Huh-uh. Best thing is for you to be gone before they finish." He switched his toothpick to the other side of his mouth. "Your boy's doing a great job. He's a natural. Though if you tell 'em I said so, I'll call you a liar to your face."

Dani suppressed a smile. This guy was nothing but a teddy bear.

"Hunter's got a real chance at detective, and this first time leading the team could be his ticket. So you need to vamoose." He disappeared down the hallway.

Well, when he put it that way … she pulled out her phone and called Tasha to secure transportation.

Cal returned and attached crime scene tape across the doorway. Likely for her benefit since no one except police were in or even near the building. "I'll let Hunter know you've gone."

"And tell him I'm not upset or anything."

The all-lip smile he spread looked odd on his grizzly face. "Happy to be your messenger."

At least, that's what he said. But Jay's call the next morning confirmed that Cal only gave Jay half of the story.

"He said you left. Just like that? Not even a goodbye?"

"You were in charge." She sipped mint tea from her Big D mug. "I didn't want to make you look bad in front of the other officers."

"I get it. Cal pressed you into leaving." His tone lowered a few notches. "He wants me to move into the supervisor job that's opening up."

"He doesn't want it?"

"Too much responsibility, to hear him talk about it."

"He said you were going to be a detective." She opened her laptop and logged on.

"My dad's a detective, though he's at a smaller town. I guess I've always had that as a goal because of him."

"Don't you enjoy what you do now?" She knew he did. The way he lit up when he showed her the three-dimensional data proved his passion.

"I do, but I'd love to do more than simply collect the information. I want to help analyze it, actually put the pieces of the puzzle together instead of simply turning them all over."

She could understand that. No fun in watching others put together a jigsaw. "Seems a shame though. You're already excellent at what you do."

"Thanks. That's why I'm interested in the supervisor's position. He does both, like a go-between. Leads a scene crew, but he also works with the detectives assigned to the case, so he gets to be in on both processes."

"The best of both." She opened her news feed to the Dallas update. "A blend of what you do well and what you're passionate about."

"I think I'd like the job. If I can get it. Cal seems to think I should."

"He's interesting, your partner." She sipped her tea again. "On the outside, all crust and concrete, but inside he's sweet and mushy. Like a toasted marshmallow."

"Burnt more like."

"And with that toothpick he keeps in his mouth, he's even skewered." Dani giggled and took another sip of tea.

Jay chuckled. "He finally gave up smoking, and chewing on them helps."

"That's it." She set her cup down before she spilled on her keyboard.

"Smoking?" He paused. "I don't get—."

"No, the toothpick. That was the other thing in the drawer that shouldn't have been closed. The thing I couldn't remember that I saw at Albert's desk. There was a toothpick inside the drawer. An orange one. Darkened on one end like it had been used and was still a little damp."

Silence. Did he not understand?

"That could be the reason the killer came back into the cube to leave. He or she had dropped a toothpick and didn't have time to grab it before Carla came in."

"If it was used, then there is likely DNA still in that desk drawer."

"After your cleaning?"

Her face heated. "I … it was closed. We don't usually clean inside closed drawers." She huffed. "I mean, I did look in it again. Enough to be sure of my memory, but if I'd cleaned it up, you couldn't go check for residue."

"It doesn't quite work like that. I mean I can. In fact, I probably will if you'll tell me where the toothpick was, but the analysts have to have a suspect to compare the DNA to. And we just lost the prime one."

"They released his ex-wife?" As they should have. Something about the mom with two kids didn't strike her as a killer.

"Right. Preliminary findings connect the two murders. Thanks to your observations."

"Don't short-change yourself, Sherlock. You've got the cool new toy. I'd never have thought of the ceiling if the messed up tile wasn't staring me in the face."

"Either way, the guess is that the perpetrator entered elsewhere in the building and used the braces in the upper crawl-space to move to a chosen location where he surprised his victim."

"I'm amazed that those pieces of flimsy metal can hold anything bigger than a rat." Of course, she wasn't an expert.

"Not the ones at the Judith Albright Center. Reinforced, like they were made for hurricanes or something."

"Up here?" Tornadoes, possibly.

"Strange, I know, but they were strong enough to hold me up. With about four feet of space, moving around the building wasn't even hard. Or noisy."

The killer could have been all over the building while they were sitting there. "Yikes."

"Let it go, Dani. You done good."

But the crime wasn't solved. "If what you're saying is all true, we could have a serial killer on our hands."

"Not on your hands. But that term has come up." He cleared his throat. "Officially though, comparison indicates the same person. Nothing more."

"A maintenance guy and a marketing associate. What do they have in common?"

"Not my area of expertise. If nothing else, they both worked at buildings by the same architectural company, and thank you for pointing out the similarities."

She opened her internet and Googled architectural companies in Dallas. "Who was the architect?"

He paused. "Why?"

Why? Duh! She set her gaze on the ceiling for a second. "I wonder how many other buildings they've designed."

"Shall I remind you that I'm not a detective and you're not even a cop?"

"I can find out." She might not have all of the resources that her dad had, or all of his connections since she was lying low, but she could glean information with the best. She opened a search page for Dallas architects and fed in the Judith Albright Center. "My dad taught me a lot about research."

"For evidence that gets thrown out of court?"

"I'm remaining within the law." She knew where the edges were. "I'm not ignorant of such things."

The silence lingered a second more. "I wish you wouldn't, Dani. You don't need to insert yourself into the investigation like this. People who do that usually end up putting themselves, and the cops who have to save them, into danger."

She flinched remembering how he'd been shot a month ago, trying to help her against a desperate person. "But what if I can learn something important? I already have, haven't I?"

"Yes, because you were a witness. But continuing to investigate isn't part of that issue."

And she was no longer on the witness list. Maybe he hadn't realized that yet. Full stop. She couldn't risk his questions to simply satisfy her curiosity. "I see what you mean." She let enough resignation into her tone to give him the feeling of compliance, but she hadn't made her mind up yet.

Once she got off the phone with him, she had to check out one more bit of information.

Chapter Ten

Jay had spent the weekend working up his scan analysis, building the 3-D digital model, and submitting his reports, but something continued to nag at him.

He sat as his desk filtering out the Monday morning conversations, the ringing telephones, scraping chairs, and belligerent detainees.

"What's bugging you?" Cal leaned back in his desk chair.

"Mind-reading?" Jay opened the digital file and clicked to Winnie Theisen's statement.

"You tend to stare a lot when things don't add up." After their years together, Cal should know.

"These two murders. The only thing holding them together is the location."

"And the killer's access." Cal pointed at the ceiling. "But what I don't get is why Theisen was even there. He rarely worked late, according to his office-mate."

Office-mate being Carla. "That was covered from his date book, though." Jay pulled up the report on Winnie Theisen's interview. "According to the book, his ex-wife was coming by to talk about schooling for the boys."

"No wonder she was suspect prime." Cal turned toward his desk. "But this isn't your case anymore, Hunter. Why are you even interested?"

He was right. What was it about this case? "Maybe because it hits close to home. Carla's still on the suspect list, though not too high, thankfully."

"And your lady found the body."

Not exactly, but not worth the correction. "Anyway, Winnie cancelled via text message." He scanned the report. "Said her boyfriend insisted she stay at the house with the kids and make a home-cooked meal."

"Only the kids were playing down the street. Yeah, I got it right here." Cal tapped his foot against the platform of his chair. "She and the boyfriend both knew Albert was on site. But have you seen the woman? Short and a little bulky. She'd never be able to get up and down through the tiles."

Jay tapped his pen on his desk. "You know what I don't like, though? Ralph Canzonari's murder was sloppy."

"Broken tile. Destroyed table. A literal shout that it was a copycat." Cal pulled a toothpick from his desk dispenser and tucked it into his teeth.

"Exactly." Jay pointed the pen at him, then let his gaze drift to the floor. "I know it's impossible, but I still like Darren Balducci for this."

"Okay …." Cal folded his arms. "He would be the number one guy to gain from the second murder. Otherwise, Winnie gets nothing but convicted and jailed."

"But, he was in Austin when Theisen was killed." Jay slammed the pen to his desk.

"So she inherits and they both win."

And get off scot-free.

Cal leaned forward and checked a note on his desk. "By about thirty mil."

Jay picked up his jacket. "Unless we can poke some holes in that impenetrable alibi. You up for a scene visit?" He didn't wait for Cal's answer but headed toward the exit.

He had a desk drawer he needed to swab.

Dani stacked the broken pieces of the table leg into the open box on the floor of the tutoring center. As she added sections of the broken leg , dirt particles bounced on the carpet. "Wow, this is just one day's filth?"

Tasha shrugged. "The place houses kids. What do you expect?"

Well, she had expected to get most of the afternoon off. Unlikely at this point.

"I don't think this table is worth attempting a reconstruct." Tyrone held metal pieces in one hand and talked on his cell phone in the other. He dumped the pieces into his upside-down helmet.

"He'll have to start from scratch on most of the corners." Tasha pulled her mask down. She hauled over the broken section of the table surface. "Except this one." She laid it surface down in the box. "Junk yard bound."

Tyrone hung up and joined them. "I finally got Frank to accept my reasoning when I told him how many hours it would take me to rebuild."

"Good for Frank." Dani released a handful of bolts to scatter across the bottom of the box. If only she could solve her conflict about what to tell Jay as easily.

She'd only searched a few sites after their phone call. Not more than an hour. Surely, he'd not be ticked about that.

But what she'd learned might open new evidence. If only she could make the final connection.

"Masks." Tyrone moved the last of the table over, exposing the stained area of the carpet.

Dani manned the utility knife and cut a wide rectangle. While Tyrone rolled the section up and moved it to a plastic covering for treatment, she set to removing every atom of residue from the exposed cement.

As lunch neared, she finally approved of the cement but still hadn't decided on when to tell Jay what she had learned. Not yet. She needed real proof to solidify her suspicion. Her dad had always taught her, "Your gut can only get you so far. Then you have to buckle down and do the legwork to support your theories."

And that's what she had—a high pile of ideas and possibilities, but nothing concrete to tie it all down. One stiff breeze and her hypothesis tumbled.

What she needed was a few answers from a key person. Innocent queries. Jay couldn't get mad about that.

"Can we take a little longer than normal for lunch?" Dani slipped out of her protective gear and whipped the goggles off her face.

Tasha smirked. "Got a date with a cop?"

"With a cop? A po-lice-man?" Tyrone stretched out the word. "Now who could that be?"

"I didn't say that. I only asked if I could take about an hour and a half." She shrugged. "I have an … errand." They could toy with that all they wanted.

"Gee. I want to have an errand." Tasha tucked her hands under her chin and batted her eyelashes. "Tall and muscle-bound with dark hair and intense eyes. Or blond and laughing. I'm not particular."

Dani lifted her gaze to the sky. Jay's eyes were more tender than intense and often filled with laughter. Wait, where had that thought come from?

Tyrone spread a wide smile. "Seriously, we're way ahead of the schedule. If you guys want to stretch the lunch hour, sounds good to me. And Frank won't say a word about it. Not if I'm the one who tells him."

It wasn't like they'd charge for the hours they didn't work.

"As long as we finish before five, nobody cares." He shed his protective suit and followed them out the door.

Dani locked it behind them. She'd be sure to get back first.

Plugging the address she'd found into her GPS, Dani followed the directions to a nearby suburb. Nice house. Large and well-manicured on the outside. About what she'd envisioned for Albert Theisen. But she hadn't expected a couple of kids fiddling with a rocket out in the cul-de-sac as she parked at the curb. Why weren't they in school?

"Is that thing loaded?" She eyed the adolescent boys, both with rather round faces.

"Duh. Yes." The taller one rolled his striking blue eyes.

Why did kids feel the need to treat everyone around them as stupid? Then again, maybe she was. She'd come out here, hadn't she? Alone? Jay would have her head if he found out. Which he wouldn't … probably.

"Do you live here?" She pointed at the address she'd been seeking.

They whispered something between themselves. Maybe they were wary of stranger danger? Mmm, nah. They were simply being boys.

She locked her door and tucked the key fob into her purse. "That thing isn't going to hit my car is it?"

"Heck, no." The taller one spoke again, but Dani didn't like the way the little one smirked.

She turned toward the light-colored house. A mottled brick, white-toned with brownish accents.

Color. Seemed like most of the houses around here were in shades of brown and cream. No bright yellows, blues, cherry reds, or greens like she'd grown up with. Not to her taste anyway. But then again, they matched everything else her life had become. Subdued.

She rang the doorbell. A short refrain of The Eyes of Texas followed. The door opened to reveal a woman, Winnie Theisen? "Yes?" She stood in the doorway. Same dark hair and bright eyes as the kids in the street.

Dani blinked. She'd rehearsed her whole spiel. But now, facing the short, round woman, she remembered none of her plan. "I'm Dani. Foster. Dani Foster." Whoa. That had not been part of her intention.

"If you're selling something, Ms. Foster, I'm not in the market." She leaned back, letting the door drift closed.

"No, no. I'm not selling anything. I wanted to share my condolences over the death of your ex-husband, Mrs. Theisen." This better be Mrs.

Theisen or she'd be embarrassed. The woman hesitated and opened the door wider.

"Balducci. Darren and I were married this morning."

"Oh." Interesting. "Then, may I also offer my congratulations." There, Dani had already learned a piece of valuable information, though not the connection she needed.

"You're not police."

So she could be a door-to-door seller but not a cop? What was it about Dani that screamed amateur? "No. My friend and I found your ... Mr. Theisen."

The woman's carefully crafted eyebrow arched. "And you just came on by to tell me how sorry you were for my loss." Her harsh Texas accent dripped with sarcasm.

"This is sort of closure for me. Therapy to get over the trauma." She let her voice break ever-so-slightly, having finally found her way back to her script. "I'm trying to put the whole tragedy behind me. But you can't imagine what it's like to find a man in the last seconds of his life." Her tone rose a squeak. "I'm so sorry. I thought I could do this without crying again."

"Honey. You must've had a terrible experience." Winnie patted her back.

"Dreadful. But I don't want to drag it all up for you. Not on such a special occasion." Dani shifted gears to what she really wanted to know. "But where is your new husband?"

Winnie's mouth curved up. Her affection for Balducci showed. "He needed to check in with his boss. Make sure they didn't need him on the site."

"He works construction?"

"For now." She fingered the ring adorning her left hand. "Until my inheritance kicks in and he can quit."

"How lovely for both of you. Especially if he hates his job."

She lifted her chin. "He doesn't hate it. And he's good at it—electrical wiring. But when you don't have to work, why do it?"

"Electrical? Really? What a coincidence. My house is in the worst shape. Breakers throw every time it rains."

"That's not right." She opened the door wider and picked up a card from the entry hall table.

"Here's Darren's contact information. If he can't help you, someone at Webb Electrical can."

"I'm glad I came by then." Glad indeed. She took the card. At least she'd learned what she came for.

Winnie glanced down toward the street and shook her finger at the boys. "I told y'all to go to the back yard with that thing."

The older one stood from where he'd been adjusting his rocket. "It's too bumpy back there. The rocket won't stand straight."

Dani glanced at the launch pad on the other side of the roadway. Even on asphalt, the pointed tube didn't look exactly straight. In fact, from where Dani stood, it seemed to be leaning … toward her car. "Hey, wait."

With a puff of ignition the white cone flared and shot off of its stand, spiraling a bit until it hit the base of the Honda's windshield.

"My car!"

The boys giggled and ran toward the creek on the other side of the cul-de-sac. Dani raced down the incline to survey the damage, a pinprick of a hole with about a half-inch spider web of cracked glass surrounding it. Grr. She picked up the rocket from where it lay against her windshield wiper. "How could such a little thing pack a punch like that?"

Winnie joined her, taking a closer look from the driver's side. "It's hardly even noticeable. Barely a spot." Her nonchalant words didn't match the scarlet creeping up her neck.

The woman clearly hoped to avoid taking responsibility for her kids' actions. No wonder they ran off. "A crack like this will only spread."

"Then you probably need to have it repaired." A male voice sounded from behind her, making her jump. She whirled and looked up into the sun. She could make out little about him except that he was tall. Built like a telephone pole. "There's a place down the road a ways. A car wash. Can't remember the name. Right before Trinity Mills." He moved toward Winnie, giving Dani a view of dark hair and hard eyes. He pulled a toothpick from his mouth. "They give a discount if you wash your car at the same time." He smiled and put his arm around his wife.

Staring at his toothpick, Dani froze. Orange.

Exactly like the one she'd seen in Albert Theisen's open desk drawer.

He flicked it into the grass behind him, and she let it drop from her sight, maintaining eye contact. "I'll … give it … a try." She fumbled to get her keys out of her purse and pressed the panic button accidentally. Her car alarm sounded and all three of them jumped.

"Turn that thing off." The woman pressed her hands against her ears.

Dani tore her eyes from the man and punched the unlock button.

"No harm done." He spread out a lipless smile showing slightly crooked but whitened teeth. "Miss …?"

"Fo …" She flinched like she'd been slapped. "I … have to go." She struggled to open her door but pounced on the lock button the moment she sat down. She tried to muster a smile at the couple. They stared at her through her broken windshield. She still clutched the rocket piece. Dropping it into the passenger seat, she shifted the car to reverse, and backed at least five yards away before she made the U-turn.

The boys hid behind a neighbor's car. She caught sight of their laughter and pointing as she drove off. No matter. Their troubles were so much bigger than hers. And it stank that two young boys would have to go through all they had endured and be stuck with a creep like their stepfather. Or was he their real father? Either way, she did nothing but pity them.

She eyed the card she'd received from Winnie. At least something good had come from this trip.

Chapter Eleven

Jay had indeed found some type of dried liquid in the drawer at Ingersol. Surely it would finally give a more reasonable focus to these cases. After dropping off the sample at the lab, he headed for the Judith Albright Center.

Dani's team was completing their packing when he arrived.

"Thought we were going to miss you this time, Officer Hunter." Tasha giggled. "Even though you delayed us an hour and a half."

"I did? What do you mean?"

"We could have finished without Dani."

Tyrone bumped his fist against Jay's outstretched one. "But then she would have missed an afternoon of pay."

"Where was Dani?" Where is Dani? He glanced around and spotted her carrying a duffel bag from the center.

Tyrone leveled a knowing look at him. "What, you can't tell your best friend you finally achieved dating status with that lady?"

What was he talking about? "I've tried twice, Ty. Both epic fails."

"Until lunch." Tasha cocked an eyebrow at him, but with his silence, her smile dropped away.

Jay watched Dani's trek across the lot until she stopped at the back of the van and shoved the bag inside.

She strolled toward the group. "I guess Tyrone told you to check off another successful site investigation."

Silence met her declaration. Jay scrutinized her face. Where had she been, and why would she tell her friends she was out with him?

She glanced from face to face through the silence.

Ty finally broke it open. "Where did you go at lunch if you didn't go out with Jay?"

"I thought you were meeting him at some restaurant." Tasha put her hands on her hips.

Dani pinked. "I didn't say anything about Jay or a date or even eating."

She was investigating again. The way she avoided his eyes confirmed it. He turned away from the group.

"I had an errand. I told you …."

A crack on her windshield drew his attention. "An errand where you caught a flying rock? Or was it a bat?"

"It's not what you think." She followed him.

Tasha and Ty joined them near her car.

"It was only a couple of kids. Boys playing with a rocket. The crazy thing flew right at my window."

Sounded dumb enough to be true.

"The parents are paying to fix it, right?" Ty lightly touched the surface of the glass.

"Well, it was sort of an accident."

"Still, they should pay for it. Or better yet, make the boys pay for it." Tasha went back to the van and climbed the ladder to the base of the cargo hold.

Dani's neck held reddish blotches instead of the fetching blush from before. "I didn't see it as necessary."

"Did they bully you?" Ty balled up his hands. "I'll go out there with you—"

"No." Her shout practically advertised she was keeping something back. Something big. And something Jay wanted to hear about. Away from Ty and Tasha.

"Look, since we didn't get that lunch, why don't we go for some now?"

"Now?" She leveled her gaze at the asphalt.

He turned his back on the others and glared at

her.

With the pregnant pause, she glanced up at him.

"I'm thinking burgers." He arched his eyebrow.

Her eyes widened. She straightened. "I could go for a burger."

Dani turned and threw her car keys up to Tasha. "Be careful."

She followed Jay to his Charger and climbed into the passenger seat. "Okay. What's this all about?"

"Lunch." Amazingly, he got the one word forth without erupting. Breathe. Getting angry wouldn't get him answers.

"I'm really not hungry."

"Of course you are. You didn't have lunch, remember?" He kept his tone even, but judging from her stiffened spine, she'd definitely caught the irritation in his voice.

He pulled onto the street, spotting a

Whataburger sign at the next intersection. He headed that direction and pulled into the lot. "How do you like your burgers?"

"I really don't—"

"Yes?"

She growled and slumped into the seat. "Cheese and no onions."

Pulling to the sign, he made the order.

"And a Diet Dr Pepper." She paused. "And ... fries."

Finishing her order, he duplicated it for himself and collected the food from the window. He drove into the street then turned east onto Northwest Highway. He kept his lips pressed together and avoided looking at her.

Good thing she didn't push a conversation. He might have told her what he thought of her deception before he could fully calm himself. He took his parcels and passenger to Winfrey Point, pulling past the baseball diamonds to the high place on the eastern shore of White Rock Lake. The sparse clouds and descending sun were showing God's finger paints on the sky across the forefront of the Dallas skyline. This was the quiet spot he craved.

Leaving his food and Dani, Jay climbed out and leaned against the front of his car.

God, everything about this woman ties me in knots. How do I talk to someone whose word I can't trust? He looked across the several miles to the glass skyscrapers reflecting the orange and pink of the sun.

And why couldn't he trust her? She hadn't spoken lies. Not to him or about him. But she'd allowed people to believe wrongly. Same deception without actual words.

She emerged from his Charger and joined him at the front. "Are we going to talk or sit separately and stay angry?"

"Look, Dani. I'm ticked. I'll get over it, but I don't like being deceived … or ignored."

"And I don't like being pressed into making

promises … which I didn't make, by the way." A spark in her eyes distracted him, but only for a moment.

"No, but you led me to believe we were in agreement. You had no intention of leaving this case alone."

She turned away and flailed her arms. "How could I? You weren't going to do anything. Remember the I'm not a detective speech?"

His face heated. "I remember. The point was that you didn't need to be doing any investigating."

"But I only wanted to check on something." Her shoulders slumped. "I had a hunch. If I'd been wrong, I would have stopped, like you asked, but I was in the middle of trying to figure out a puzzle."

"And you figured it out?" Could this finally be the end of her searching for clues and answers?

Her dark eyes lit with a fire. "I did. I found the architects. Their website specifically advertises load-bearing ceiling braces resistant to high winds."

"I already know that."

She wandered back to her door and opened it. "I'm sure there are a lot of other buildings that have ceilings like that, though." She snagged the bags of food.

Might as well encourage her a little. "Not as many as you think. Older ones might, but the newer ones are usually built cheap and chic, not always ultra-sturdy." He followed suit, grabbing a blanket from his back seat along with their drinks. "Shall we sit?"

She eyed him for a moment, chewing on a fry. Tilting her head, she shrugged and helped him.

He waited until she settled on the blanket with a blue-jeaned knee propping up one elbow and took a bite of her sandwich. "That doesn't explain who decorated your windshield."

Her face caught the glow of the sunset as she stared across the lake. High cheekbones accented her graceful jawline and neck. A wisp of hair escaped the bun on the back of her head. The tuft nuzzled against her smooth, creamy skin until she pushed it behind her ear.

He looked away for a second and steered his mind from the distraction of her beauty. "Who were the boys, Dani?"

Her eyes shifted to his, but he didn't smile. Not this time. Guilt painted her face, and she dropped her gaze to the grass in front of her outstretched sneaker.

"Where did you go?"

"I wanted to meet Winnie Theisen. Winnie Balducci. They got married this morning."

"Are you out of your mind?" Why did this woman insist on constantly putting herself in dangerous predicaments? He shut his eyes against her pout and took a deep breath.

"I thought maybe I could chat with her a bit, woman to woman." She held out a business card. "And I connected her new husband to the building architects."

He took the card and stared at it. Webb

Electrical. "Darren Balducci?"

She nodded. "He works for a contractor. I called the receptionist there for references, and she mentioned Myerson-Cambridge Architectural Firm."

Brilliant work, but for a detective. "You're not on this case, Dani."

"I only wanted to put that piece in place."

Should he believe her? He tucked the card in his pocket and tried to relax. Taking a handful of fries from his bag, he chomped a few. "Did you learn anything else?"

"I … well, everything happened so fast, and I came back here." Her eyes drifted to the bag in her hands. She folded the top edge over on itself and rolled it over and over around the food inside.

He froze. Withholding facts. A virtual marquee scrolled the words through his mind. How did he draw the truth out of her when she had no hint of sharing? "And you came back with a broken windshield?"

"That's about the size of it. I'm sorry I didn't listen to you." Her refusal to meet his gaze practically trumpeted untold secrets.

"But you learned something else?" He lifted his brows. "About Theisen's murder?"

Her mouth dropped open. "How did you know?"

"I'm the one who's supposed to investigate." He took a bite of his sandwich and washed it down the back of his throat with a swig of his soda. Still, Dani hadn't offered what she learned. "Okay, let's play twenty questions. Did Winnie say something about her husband?"

She stared off at the now-dark lake and shook her head slightly. "It wasn't her."

"You didn't meet her after all?"

"No." She fidgeted. "I met her, all right. And also … I think I know who killed Albert Theisen."

Chapter Twelve

With the sun fully set, the darkness enveloped the overlook and completely hid Jay's expression. He had to be furious. And he should be after she'd ignored his request to stay out of the investigation.

As much as she wanted to leave out her encounter with Darren Balducci, she couldn't keep hiding things from Jay. Not if she cared about him. "I didn't think I'd lay eyes on the man."

"That's right, you didn't think." He stood quickly and moved to his trunk.

What now?

A moment later, he returned with a standing

floodlight that he aimed at the car. The reflected light dimly illuminated both of them and their near surroundings. "Obviously you think Balducci is the prime suspect."

"Unless it is some serial killer."

He gave her a side-long glance. His tone and facial features had eased a bit.

"But then, your office doesn't want to use that word." A smile tugged at her lips.

"The detectives on the case, the real detectives …."

"Ouch."

He cocked his head in her direction. "They're still considering the possibility because of the similarities that you pointed out."

"What if Balducci killed him, though. And then did this crime like the other to get Winnie out of jail?" That had to be it. "Winnie can't be so lucky that the second murder was a coincidence."

"We've thought of that, too. Officially, Balducci was out of town when Albert was killed.

Unofficially, I've been trying to poke holes in his statement." He held out his hand. "Want to walk a little?"

Smiling, she took it, clutching her bag in her other hand.

"I also found some residue in Albert's drawer, right where you said it would be." He collected his light and directed it on the ground in front of them.

Yes. "Now all you need to do is a DNA check."

"Not so easy. No sample from Balducci. And he's not likely to just offer us one."

Her mind ripped back to the toothpick he'd been chewing. The one he'd so casually tossed. Should she share that with Jay? What if they couldn't find it? Then she'd be embarrassed and he'd be humiliated in front of his co-workers.

"But you think he could have come back from Austin?"

"I have nothing to base that on." He slowed his walk. "A feeling. Why would a guy order enough food for two or three meals and prepay for a dozen in-room movies?"

"So he can have an alibi?"

He shrugged. "If I could only find one ounce of evidence to support my gut." Glancing at her, the inklings of his smile drifted away. "If we're right about this, you came face to face with a murderer."

"He has no reason to give me a second thought. I didn't even give him my name when he asked."

His eyes widened. "Balducci asked for your name?"

"Only in a random way. Talked about where to get my windshield fixed."

Fully stopping on the trail, he whirled to face her. "I don't like it. I don't like that he's seen your face, fished for your name, or saw your license plate. If he wants to find you, he can."

The compassion in his dark eyes touched her. She squeezed the hand she held. "Why would he? I said nothing to him."

"If we're on the right track, he didn't even know his second victim." He brought her fingers to his lips. "I don't want to see you in danger. Not again."

She smiled. Jay was such a good guy. "Okay. I'll hang up my Sherlock Holmes cap."

"I'm Sherlock, remember?" Keeping her hand close to his chest, he continued down the trail.

"But Watson doesn't have a special hat."

He smiled and glanced back at her. "Yeah, but she's a special lady." He led her up an incline. "This is one of my favorite places. You know how Jesus would get alone and spend time with the Father? This is my spot."

"It's lovely." Made even sweeter by the man whose company she enjoyed.

"Another week or two and the fields we parked by will be full of ball games. Little League and softball groups of all ages." He veered around a spider web in the making, stretched between two trees.

She paused and released him in order to watch the web builder. "Do you play?"

He directed the beam at the creature. "Our department had a team last year. I guess they will again. Sort of a tradition, you know?"

Tradition, yes. Full of fond memories. "My … uh." Dad had played for years on the team for his department. But that ventured into the area of things she wasn't supposed to speak of. She'd already said too much about her father, but how could she redirect the conversation?

"Did you play when you were younger?"

"No. I liked to watch, though." That should do it. She tried to make her tone light, though it sounded strained even to her ear.

"Your dad?"

She flinched. "What about him?" Ach. Way to be subtle. This was what keeping secrets and lying to people she liked did to her.

"Did you watch your dad play?" He led her higher up the hill.

"Oh." Duh. She rolled the top of her food bag and held it tight. "A little."

"What does he do now?"

How had their conversation veered toward her father? "Why do you want to know about my dad?"

At a level place, he slowed to a stop. "I can't shake the feeling that there's a reason your name disappeared from the witness list. The captain led me to believe it was because of political clout." He switched the light to his other side and turned toward her. "Is there something you're not telling me?"

She squirmed. A lot of somethings. How did she get away from this topic? "Have you always had issues with trusting people?" Attacking Jay was the last thing she wanted to do, but she had to redirect him somehow.

He dropped his chin. "Habit." His gaze lifted with a slight shake of his head. "A bad one."

"Do you suspect me of something?"

"No." He lifted his open palm. "I'm doing this poorly. I'm sorry, Dani. I thought maybe your dad was a senator or judge …."

"My father's dead." More than she'd wanted to say, but at least he wouldn't ask again.

Regret painted his expression as his gaze locked with hers. "I really am sorry. No wonder you came here to sort of start over."

His sensitive eyes mesmerized her. She let them suck her in for a moment until his words connected. Start over. Wait. He was getting too close to the truth. She broke the connection and headed up the hill again.

"For the record, I don't know any politicians." She reached the top and paused as he joined her. She stared at the zipper edge of his police jacket. "Without trust … well, there's not much of a relationship that can be had."

Of course, she wasn't trustworthy. And she sure didn't deserve an amazing guy like Jay.

"It's not that I don't trust you." He took a few steps alone toward an outcropping, once again facing the lake. Then he turned. "This whole thing is odd. You know I don't like untied threads."

Marji Laine

So much so he had to double check every crime scene she'd ever cleaned up for him. *Oh, God, this is such a good guy. If You've brought us together, how can I discard what You might be building?*

He was worth her effort. If he ever did find out about her, he'd walk away, no doubt. But until that time, if it ever did come, she wanted to be his Watson.

Releasing a long exhale, she closed the gap between them. "If you can get over untied threads, I can certainly overlook regrettable questions of the past."

He slipped his empty hand into hers. "I guess I can live with that."

This sure felt like a date, though it had started all wrong. Maybe it would end well. But then, considering their history of almost-dates, anything less than a car crash or another crime scene call would be a success.

She hadn't reckoned on Tasha's grocery run, though. The blonde was juggling too many bags when Jay pulled into the lot. Dani jumped out and grabbed a breaking bag before a jug of milk hit the asphalt. "Let me help you."

Jay joined them, closing the hatch as he unloaded the last of the packages.

"I thought I could get them all, but I didn't expect the bags to break." Tasha led the way upstairs.

"It's all right. Good timing." Or maybe bad timing, considering the closeness she and Jay had enjoyed.

The three unloaded at the kitchen table. Jay pulled his keys from his pocket. "I should go, left my door open downstairs." He pivoted toward the entrance.

"I had a nice time."

"Me, too." His eyes held hers a moment, then he touched her chin. "No more investigating."

"Scout's honor." She held up three fingers, though she'd only been a Brownie for a year.

With that enchanting half-smile of his, he

turned away.

Leaning against the closed door, she reflected on his touch, his smile, his …. No. Had she promised him? How could she let him down again, but how could she not?

Jay braced his phone against his cheek. Seemed the same song kept playing and playing. He set his phone on the desk and punched the speaker button, then he refocused on his monitor. A list of recent unsolved murders. Two others had been in buildings constructed by Myerson-Cambridge Architects along with Theisen's and Canzonari's.

He flipped from one report to the next as Cal sauntered up carrying a French pastry, the crumbs of which decorating the front of his dark-blue dress shirt. "Bags are growing under your eyes, Hunter. People are gonna start thinking you're the old man and I'm the kid."

Jay leaned back and rubbed his face before taking the Starbucks cup that his partner held out.

"How long ya been here?"

"Couple of hours. Couldn't get back to sleep." Not after what he'd learned from Dani started visiting his dreams.

"All right, let's have it." Cal pulled a chair closer and peered over Jay's shoulder at the computer.

"I'm not sure what I have. Maybe nothing. Maybe something." He took a sip from the brew and angled his primary monitor so Cal could see it. "Starting with the copycat …."

Cal leaned back in the swivel chair. "Winnie got off, and Balducci gets to absorb her inheritance."

"As her new hubby."

He cocked an eyebrow in Jay's direction. "Really."

"And he'd be set, except for the toothpick Dani

saw in the drawer at Ingersol. Looks like Balducci dropped it out of his mouth while he was killing Theisen ...."

"Excuse me?" Cal straightened and raised his finger.

"Right, suspected of dropping and killing."

"Filthy habit." Cal licked the finger and scooped up some of the sugar flecks from his shirt.

"If we're right, he's done one copycat. I focused on the architects, Myerson-Cambridge, to look for others." He clicked the other monitor to the listing on the builder's website.

"All these buildings were designed by the same company?" Cal let the strudel in his right hand do the pointing. "So many of them. There's bound to be a few on the murder listing."

"Yeah, but four? Each separated by exactly one weekend?"

"The boys are already contemplating serial." Cal lowered his voice on the last word.

A hint of that would make national news

within the hour.

"Not exactly my slant." Jay puffed an exhale. "After I talked to Dani last night, I needed to check on Balducci again."

"Dani? Last night?" He clasped his hands. "Well, well, well."

"What did you say about people thinking I'm the adult and you're the child?"

Cal growled. "Okay, keep moving."

"That's as far as I've gotten. I'm waiting …." The music halted, and Jay grabbed for the phone.

"Are you still there?" Was this the same voice as before? Hard to remember that far back.

"This is Specialist Jay Hunter from Dallas. I need to speak to the concierge who worked …."

"Yes, sir. I was the one on duty that night."

Good. "I have a few questions about the guest in your room 406, Darren Balducci."

"To my knowledge, except for the room service that afternoon, no one saw or spoke to him."

"And the room service." Jay read from a list in

the file. "An appetizer, steak and potato, quesadilla, fajitas …."

"Big appetite." Cal's eyebrows lowered, and his lip curled downward. "He can claim he munched on it all day."

"Nothing to drink? Water bottles and mini-fridge contents were all accounted for."

The concierge paused. "Hmm. Nothing ordered. And nothing was missing, but he could have brought something with him."

Maybe there'd been a cup in the trash can? "Can I speak to the housekeeping supervisor?" The music clicked on again.

Jay swiveled his seat to face Cal. "Wonder how long it'll take this time."

His partner smirked and stuffed the last of his breakfast into his mouth.

Almost immediately, the music clicked off. "I understand you have some questions, but I don't have a lot of time." A woman's voice. Direct.

He asked about the trash and the wrappers on

the glasses for the night of the Theisen murder.

"Just a moment, let me check my record." The line went silent, but thankfully, the music didn't return. A moment later, she was back on the line.

No glasses were used and no cups were left out. A good answer, but that still didn't give enough reason to believe he'd left the hotel.

Then she started explaining something else. A smile initiated at his toes and spread upward. He took the woman's name, thanked her and hung up.

Cal eyed him. "Let me guess. His bed was still neat."

"Nope." He lifted his chin. "But the supervisor mentioned a leak. A toilet next door flooded and seeped through the wall to the floor of Balducci's room. Housekeeping had to clean right around the dinner hour."

Cal leaped to his feet. "And he wasn't there." He slapped Jay on the shoulder. "I knew you had it in you, kid."

Lieutenant Gates appeared, heading toward

them.

"Wait 'til you hear, Lieutenant." Cal grinned.

Gates didn't smile. "I'll wait. Grab your gear."

Chapter Thirteen

Dani removed grunge from the blade of an ultra-fine Spackle-knife. Days without cleaning jobs came less and less often, so the team took every opportunity to give their tools a thorough scour.

She worked closer to the stairs leading from the main entrance at the top of the hill to this lower level. Tyrone and Tasha cleaned some of the bigger pieces near the cargo doors on the other side of the warehouse. Their distant chatter allowed Dani to reflect on the mess she'd made of her circumstances.

Matthew always preached at her to embrace her new life. Her concealment of her background kept her alive. She shouldn't think about the stories as falsehoods. Rather, they had become her new truth.

But as much as she tried to buy into that line of thinking, nothing within her accepted the deception. Not her heart, nor her spirit. It was one thing to pretend for a short period of time when she attempted to learn information, but playing a permanent role? Especially around people she cared about? How could she be that fake?

Maybe the discarded toothpick she'd retrieved for Jay would ease the pressure of keeping secrets from him. Though she'd broken a promise to get it. However unintended the promise had been.

She tapped her blue jean pocket that held the Ziploc baggie. Darren's toothpick had been exactly where he'd thrown it. At least now, Jay would have something to compare with the residue he found at Ingersol.

He would, once she mustered the courage to call and tell him what she'd done.

"Well? Are you coming or not?" Tasha stared at her. Tyrone stepped behind her.

"Huh?" She paused and eyed the completely clean tool she'd been rubbing.

"Time to go, chickadee." Tasha threw her woven purple shawl over her shoulders and gathered her hair from under the collar. "Day is done, you know?"

"And if you keep buffing that knife, you'll dull the blade." Tyrone grinned.

She slipped the guard on the piece and put it back in the box. "I haven't finished." She eyed a squeegee that still needed attention, and she hadn't even opened one of the cases. "You both go ahead."

"Gonna be kinda hard, since I'm in your car." Tasha knelt and grabbed a rag. "I'll give you a hand."

Dani leaned back on her heels. Her roommate had an appointment with her adviser. "Why don't you take the car to go speak to Dr. Wyatt? Then you can come back and pick me up."

"Okay, if you're sure." She stood and dropped the rag on a pile. "I won't be too long." She headed for the locker room.

"I don't like leaving you here by yourself." Tyrone stuck his fingers into his front pockets.

Dani stared up at him from where she sat on the floor. "I'm fine. You heard Tasha. She'll be right back." She flicked her rag at his ankle. "Besides, Carla will be looking for you, right?"

"Supposed to go to a Bible study tonight at the church. Why don't you join us?"

She'd love it. But church had been another item she'd had to shed. Getting involved at all, since she'd always been so active, was expressly forbidden. "I need to take a pass on that one."

"Got plans tonight? Let me guess. Jay's taking you to dinner?" He widened his grin.

"No. Nothing like that." Though she wouldn't mind another burger. "Besides, we're only friends."

For the moment.

"Uh-huh." His measured tone and raised eyebrow conveyed the opposite.

Swallowing, she directed her gaze at him. "Really." She applied as much firmness as possible to her declaration.

Tyrone's eyes narrowed. He still didn't believe her.

That was all right. He didn't have to. Aside from a little hand-holding, which still made her swoon to think about, Jay hadn't given her reason to believe they were more.

He cocked his eyebrow at her. "Well, okay. I'll leave you to it, then." He winked and exited.

She went back to the case in front of her.

"See you in a bit." Tasha waved at her from the upper level balcony and disappeared.

Silence closed in around Dani. Being alone had never bothered her, but after the last couple of weeks, her mind danced through the horrifying scenarios she'd almost witnessed. Maybe staying here alone hadn't been her best idea.

Of course, she didn't have to sit in the warehouse. Several box trucks and trailers shared the floor with crated furniture waiting to be returned to their owners. Not that anyone hid there, but from the upper floor, she'd have a great view.

She stuck the bottle of cleaning supplies in the case, hoisted the whole thing into her arms, and trotted up the steps.

The only view better than the balcony was from the cherry-picker—if it was raised. That or one of the service ladders on the four columns that held up the roof. But she could see clearly that no one hid on the lower floor.

Setting the box down, she strolled into the locker room for a stack of paper towels. Taking a detour on her way back, she stopped by her locker to get some change for the soda machine. Maybe some caffeine would eliminate the impact of her dream-filled night.

As she reached to open her locker, the back of

her neck reacted like a bolt of lightning had a bead on her. She didn't exactly hear a sound outside the entrance but felt a presence. She halted and listened, but someone could easily enter and have her in full view without any warning.

Unless she could figure out a way to disappear. She glanced up. The ceiling was low in here, on-level with the rest of the building, but who knew if it was strong enough to hold her. A metallic ping from outside sounded like someone had stopped at her case of tools.

Her chest tightened as she leaped onto the bench and shoved the tile above her upward. Silently, she opened her locker and used the shelf inside as an extra boost. She grabbed the nearest brace and pulled herself through the ceiling.

With her toe, she pushed the locker door almost closed. She strengthened her grip on the vertical beam before laying the tile back into place. She expected pitch darkness, but dim light seeped in from somewhere. Enough to see the nearby braces and allow her to move.

The locker room door creaked as it opened, sending a shiver creeping across her shoulders and down her spine. Could it be Tyrone or Tasha coming back? Or a member of another team who forgot something they needed this weekend?

Possibly, but she wasn't about to go back down. Not here anyway. Descending near the front door was a better idea. There was a Burger King down the block where she could borrow a phone. She aimed that direction and duck-stepped slowly from one bracket to another.

"I know you're here, Dani Foster."

Dani froze for an instant, but the entrance was still some distance. She slowed her pace, making sure each step was silent.

"Surprised I know your name? Ha. Winnie tells me everything." The door of a locker swung open and banged against the wall behind her. "You shoulda left things alone. Shoulda stayed away."

Another locker opened. "You hiding in there?"

Balducci let out a wicked cackle that erupted the nerve endings along her arms.

She reached for the next brace closer to safety. The locker room door squealed again. Balducci had gone back out? She hesitated. Should she return?

Ahead of her a tile pushed upward. She veered to her right and picked up speed.

A tiny beam, like a small flashlight, whipped around the crawlspace. "I know you're up here. You can't hide from me."

She kept moving, but the light caught her.

"There you are." He laughed again, like something from a science fiction movie.

Without hesitation, she pushed forward. The light disappeared. He'd be much faster on the floor, but if her calculations were correct, she was nearly to the balcony. Her breath came in soft puffs, barely overwhelming the loud thump in her chest.

"Boo." The sound from behind her accompanied the illumination again.

She flinched and pressed on. Again darkness

enveloped her, but the light returned almost immediately. He'd climbed up behind her. Too close. And with a lamp, he'd have no problem overtaking her.

Tiny pricks of light appeared in front of her as she stepped onto the next bracket. The tiles didn't fit snuggly around the curve of the column. So she'd made it to the warehouse? The thought of how high she was knotted her stomach.

"Here kitty, kitty, kitty." A click sounded behind her. Metal. Ominous.

The column loomed. She could hide behind it for a moment. Figure out what to do. She reached for the next bracket and slipped. An explosion sounded behind her as she screamed and crashed through the thin tile.

Chapter Fourteen

Jay took a swig of the soda he'd bought on the way back to the station. His thoughts turned to Dani yet again. She'd probably have a suicide to clean up tomorrow or the day after. Wonder what she did today?

Cal followed him to the corner they shared. "That kid was too young."

Strange. His partner didn't usually let death affect him. Not like Jay, but at least he had prayer to fall back on. And he'd already lifted up the mother of the poor girl who had slit her wrists. "Don't let it eat at you. Isn't that what you've always told me?"

His partner sat at his desk, his back to Jay. "Not an easy thing to do sometimes. She was too young to grasp the concept of forever."

True for most suicides. Most people for that matter. "Doc said he thought she might've been pregnant."

"Like that's an excuse?" He turned red eyes toward him. "I suppose you prayed, huh."

He nodded and lifted up another. Was the Lord opening up a door? "I prayed for the girl's mom. That she'll find some comfort."

"In your God?" Bitterness seethed with his words.

"Cal, God didn't take that girl's life."

"You've always talked about His power."

"Yeah."

"He couldn't have stopped her? Couldn't have made her realize the foolishness of her action?" He wiped the back of his hand across his nose and swiveled in his chair to face his desk.

Hard questions. Cal had something in his past that put walls up to Jay's faith, but whatever it was, he never spoke of it. "God can do anything. He's always able."

"Not willing, though. This child wasn't worth His time? Pfft." His words muffled against the folded hands near his mouth.

"Of course she was worth it to Him. It's not a question of worth. It was a question of her choice."

"And He couldn't have changed her mind." His tone lowered. "Why couldn't He have changed her mind?"

God, help me get this right. "When you were a teenager, did you ever fight with your mom or dad?"

"So?"

"Did they force you to do things?"

He went silent.

"And did you resent their insistence? Did you hate that you had no choice in the matter?"

No response.

"As much as I love my parents, I couldn't get away from them fast enough back then. I wanted to be a man. Wanted to make my own decisions, even if they were mistakes. I didn't want anyone forcing me to do anything."

"All right." His chin dipped. "I get what you're saying. God doesn't want to force people."

Jay released the exhale he'd been holding. "Something like that." He laid his palm on Cal's shoulder. "Doesn't mean He doesn't care, or that it doesn't hurt when someone makes a stupid choice. I think it must hurt Him even more than it hurts us, considering all that He's done."

Cal waved him off. "Okay, okay." He took a deep breath and flicked on his computer monitor.

Bring those words back to him, Lord. Again and again. Maybe they would resonate soon.

"Looks like the analyst found DNA traces on that swab you brought in. Perriman doesn't have a sample from Balducci, though. Durwood's trying to get a judge to give them a search warrant." Cal bounced back as though the previous discussion hadn't happened.

"I need to finish the report on the conversation I had with the housekeeping supervisor. They'll get the warrant once his alibi is gone."

"Nah. He'll just come up with something else. His wife's got beau-coups of money, and he gets to spend it all." Cal spun, frowning. "I don't suppose your God's gonna do anything about that either, is He? He's gonna let Darren take the family off to someplace with limited extradition and enjoy the rest of his life."

Jay shook his head while typing up the information he'd learned. "Sorry, my friend. I don't speak for the Lord. And I gave up trying to guess what He'd do next a long time ago."

Cal came up behind him. "Fine. Then we better help Him. What about those other murders you mentioned?"

Jay added a period to his statement and saved it to the file, then flipped to another page.

"Ginhaussen's Jewelers lost their assistant manager February eighteenth. Supposedly a robbery gone wrong, but the initial report from the cleaning woman who found the body didn't mention the broken jewelry case."

Cal stopped. "You think the owner used the man's death to claim a burglary?"

"That's exactly what he did. But he didn't admit to it until last week." Jay switched to another file. "Then on the twenty-sixth, a dry-cleaning service lost a seamstress after hours."

"Same MO." Cal looked at the screen over Jay's shoulder. He pointed at a picture of the scene. "Down to the knife wounds and the white ceiling powder. Why didn't this one float to the surface when we found Theisen?"

"Which one?" Perriman passed the desk. "Are you working on my case, Hunter?"

"Some things have come out." The last thing Jay needed was to ignite the competitive fires of guys who had already made the detective level.

"Yeah, like a jet-sized hole in Balducci's alibi." Cal explained about the leak.

"That might be enough for the warrant. What else you got?" At least he sounded interested and not ticked.

"I think there are a couple of other murders set up to try to cover Albert's."

Perriman joined Cal at Jay's shoulder. "Says here, this vic was probably offed in a drug exchange."

"Which is why no one made the connection, Einstein." Cal had the tenure that allowed him to needle the detectives. "If the kid's right, Balducci went to elaborate planning to make his wife a wealthy woman."

"Hmm." Perriman took over Jay's mouse. "Same dust from the ceiling?"

Jay pointed at the screen with the long list of buildings. "The architect designed all four places."

"The last one was on Friday," Cal chimed in. "If we're not quick enough on this, he might decide to act again."

Perriman studied the information for a moment. "With K, I guess." He stood.

Jay turned his chair a bit and stared up at him.

"What are you talking about?" Cal remained where he was, staring at the screens.

The detective pointed at the Myerson-Cambridge website. "G for Ginhaussen's Jewelers. H for High Society Dry-Cleaning. Then I for the Ingersol office and J for the Judith Albright Center." With each name, he tapped the alphabetical list on the screen. "Looks like he only has one choice if he decides to keep going."

Jay didn't wait for Perriman to make the last tap. He shoved against both men and grabbed his jacket off the back of his chair in one fluid motion.

"Find your partner and meet us there." Cal followed him to the exit.

Perriman and Durwood could come if they liked, but Jay's trip to Kellerman's had more to do with the woman he was beginning to care about than it did with their investigation. He slowed at the door and slipped his phone from his pocket.

He dialed Dani's number after he jogged to his Charger. He paused to let Cal catch up. After four rings it switched to her voice mail. He ended the call and dialed Tyrone as he climbed into the driver's seat.

"Didn't expect to hear from you. But if you're wondering, no you left no evidence behind." His friend laughed.

"Very funny." Jay cleared his throat and kept his tone light. "Did you even have a job today?"

"Nope. Cleaned at the warehouse since lunch. Amazing how the grime cakes up even though we clean on them after every job."

"I don't suppose Dani is with you."

"Nope. Left her finishing up." He chuckled. "But the way you're asking, and her being all quiet today … did y'all finally get to enjoy an evening together?"

"Something like that." Jay cranked the engine

as Cal got in beside him. "So she and Tasha are still at Kellerman?"

"If Tasha's not back, she will be before too long."

"Dani's there by herself?" Jay shifted and peeled from his parking spot.

"She might be, but she was finishing up on—"

Jay stuffed the phone in his jacket pocket without disengaging. He put the car into drive and left rubber on the pavement.

"No reason to believe your girl's in danger." Cal tightened his seat belt.

But she had a way of attracting it. And Cal didn't know that she'd met Balducci the day before. Had she done something or said something that might make him try to find her? Or maybe he was simply continuing his pattern? Or … he'd be embarrassed when he got there and found nothing to worry about.

"You're probably right." Though that didn't slow Jay down at all. "My mind is telling me that, but the rest of me is one big clanging alarm."

As she fell through the ceiling, Dani tightened her grip on the horizontal brace that she'd been clinging to. One hand slipped off but wrapped around what should have been her foothold. She dared not look down and dug her fingertips into the crease of the metal brace. She released her other hand then punched it through a tile to her left and reached for the other side of the metal brace.

She dangled for a moment, her eyes tightly shut. She forced them open and emitted an airy yelp as she closed them again. Too high. Oh, God, I'm way too high. I'll never get down. You have to help me. Then, there was the crazy with the gun somewhere behind her.

She forced herself to look around. To her right and slightly behind her was the closest column. She reached her foot back but couldn't quite touch the ladder. Shuffling an inch at a time, she scooted back along the brace. She stretched her toe out again, this time connecting. Another second and she was close enough to reach out her right hand and grab the nearest rung. She released her hold on the ceiling bar and riveted herself to the cold metal.

"Now where did you go?" A light flickered against the tile.

Her spine chilled. He still had a gun. Standing on the rung, she reached around the wide column and found a matching bar on the other side. With her arms spread wide, she shifted one foot around and pulled herself to the ladder on the opposite side of the column.

"No way." Balducci's already high voice sounded strained.

She clung to the ladder trying to make herself as thin as possible.

"You did not climb down that pole."

Another tile broke. A second later, it hit the floor.

"Well, if you can swing over to that pole, then I sure can." His tenor took on a tinny, mad tone. Like a cartoon character.

She scooted further around the column. Had he possibly seen that there was a second ladder? All he had to do was look at one of the others and he'd know there was. She peered around the edge of the cement. Balducci's feet dangled through the opening.

He'd never be able to swing to the ladder. Even Tarzan wouldn't make it, and he was a cartoon.

As she watched, the tall man lowered himself through the hole and swung backward, his gun stuffed into his waistband. She dodged back behind the column. The same cement cylinder that he was aiming for. Any second, she'd hear him catch the rung on the other side of her.

She glanced down. No not down. She jerked her chin upward. Less than thirty feet high, it might as well have been 100. She had nowhere to go except back up. The thought paralyzed her. Having looked at the distance beneath her, how could she convince her hands to release their hold?

Balducci grunted.

She braced herself.

"Dani!" She glanced toward the entrance. Jay and his partner stood on the balcony.

On the other side of the column, Darren Balducci let out a scream that ended with a sickening thud. Dani kept her eyes trained on Jay as his gaze dropped from her level to the floor. He looked back toward her. "Stay right where you are."

No problem. Well, some problem. She twisted both arms through the rung and clung to the thin metal bar with a bear hug.

Chapter Fifteen

Jay handed his phone to Cal. "See if you can get Ty to tell you how to work that lift." He pointed at the basket with the extension arm.

Cal started talking into the phone almost immediately.

A series of ropes hung on the wall behind the large machine. Jay grabbed one, swung it over his shoulder, and tackled the ladder where Dani hung like the star on a Christmas tree.

He didn't even want to know how she'd gotten up there. Especially after seeing Balducci fall. "Hang on."

"Don't worry about that. I'm lousy at coming down, remember?" Her voice shook.

The lift's engine revved. "I gotcha." Cal shoved the phone into his shirt pocket and worked the controls.

"Don't get too close to her." Jay sped his ascent to stay ahead of Cal. "Stop there, for a second."

His partner beat him to the ceiling, but Jay didn't want him any closer to Dani until he could anchor her to the ladder. He climbed the last few feet. "I've got you." He looped the rope around her waist twice and tied it off on the rung.

"Who's got you?" She looped one arm around him and grabbed the back of his shirt.

"Looks like you do." He gave her a half-grin. "Okay, Cal." He lifted his voice above the hum of the machinery and nodded to his partner. "Let's see how good a teacher Tyrone is."

The man's face tightened, eyebrows pushed firmly together and jaw clamped shut. His shoulders tensed as he inched the basket forward in tiny jerks of propulsion.

Jay turned back to Dani. "Are you all right?"

Dirt etched her pale face, but otherwise, she looked whole.

She nodded, her eyes reddened.

"Aw, honey, you're okay. I've got you." He wrapped his other arm around her as she shuddered into a sob.

The box came to a stop next to them. "It ain't pretty, but it works."

Jay detached himself from Dani long enough to step onto the rim of the lift. "Stay here, just a second." He stepped firmly into the basket, then unlashed Dani and pulled her toward him. "There you go."

She wrapped one arm around him and pressed her cheek against his shirtfront while gripping the material. He tightened his grip at her back with one hand and kept hold of the safety bar with the other.

Cal manipulated a slow, smooth descent. "The guy's definitely dead." He glanced over the edge of their moving platform. "Funny how we were talking about how God might let him get away with murder."

Not exactly funny, but he understood Cal's point. Though a man's death wasn't something to celebrate. "I have no doubt that God protected Dani."

"And Balducci got his justice, after all." Cal climbed from the basket and hopped to the floor.

Jay shut his eyes. "It's not God's wish that anyone die without Him." With the movement halted, he wrapped his other arm around Dani.

"Even a murderous, scum-covered low-life like Darren Balducci?" Cal's bitterness seethed through his tone.

Jay planted a kiss on the top of Dani's head then eyed Cal. "Who needs forgiveness more than a scum-covered low-life?"

His partner jerked around to meet his gaze. The anger in his face eased. "Never thought of it that way."

Dani released him and fished something out of her back pocket. She held out an orange toothpick contained in a Ziploc snack bag. "I know you're going to be mad."

"What did you do, Dani?"

She wagged her head as a fresh crop of tears seeped down her cheeks. "He threw it on the ground while we were talking. I went back for it this morning."

Jay blew out a loud exhale. "And he came after you." He drew her back into his embrace. What was he going to do with her?

"I don't know." She wrapped her arms around his back. "He said Winnie told him my name. Maybe he did see me."

He shut his eyes and clung to her. How close he'd come to losing …. Abruptly releasing her, he bent to look directly at her. "Do you know how much danger you put yourself in?"

She collected a broken breath. "I'm so sorry, Jay."

"Sorry's not enough. You can't do this again. Never. Not if you're going to be my girl." It had just come out, but he meant it nonetheless.

"Your ...." She smiled. "I won't."

He brushed a wisp of her hair behind her ear. "You better not." He kissed her temple. "I'd really like to keep you around for a while." He lingered near her ear, his voice dropping to a whisper.

One of her hands slipped to his collar. "I'd like that."

Slightly parted lips followed her agreement. Jay lowered slowly, breathing in her citrus scent before lightly brushing her lips. She responded to the touch, and he drifted down again into a tender kiss, long enough to let her know the depths of his feelings.

"I'm surprised Perriman and Durwood aren't here already." His partner came around the column. He glanced at them and chuckled.

Dani stiffened with a sharp exhale. "Police. Of course." She stepped back and detached her fist from his shirt. "I …." She pressed the cloth against him with her fingers.

He took her hand. "It's okay. Doesn't matter."

"No." She climbed from the lift and leaned against it.

He followed. "Wait a second."

"I have to make a phone call." She pushed off the painted metal and caught herself against a crate.

"Dani." He put his hand on her shoulder. "You need to take a few seconds."

"I have to get to my phone." She leaned into the base of the stairs and darted up them two at a time.

He followed. If her face, again paling, was any indication, she'd pass out before she reached the locker room. She stumbled as she burst through the noisy door. He stood at the entrance, keeping the door ajar with his foot. "Come sit down."

"Matthew?"

Who was Matthew?

"I know it's late. I'm sorry, but I need you."

Did the echo make the tone of her voice shakier than it really was? She gulped air. "I've had another…" She glanced in Jay's direction. "…situation."

Jay let the door close. Obviously, she didn't need his help.

Dani sat at her kitchen table and set out a clean role of gauze and tape. The subtle movements of her finger shot pain through her wounded hand. Strange that she hadn't even known she'd been cut until she'd ended her phone call with Matthew and noticed blood smears all over her phone.

Jay had blood all over his shirtfront, making him worry that she had a severe injury. And even when he learned it was only her hand, he made sure she was treated right away. He'd even taken her home and insisted on delivering her to her door.

If only he'd kissed her good night again.

Instead, he took off as soon as he made sure Tasha, who had followed from the warehouse, was planning to stay home with her.

Didn't matter. The earlier kisses had been enough to infiltrate her dreams all night. Though her injured hands awakened her earlier than she had wanted.

She removed the lid from the tube of ointment, trying to spread it without causing too much pain, when Tasha came in from an early-morning run.

"Need some assistance?" Tasha grabbed a water bottle from the fridge. She took a swig and sat across from her.

"A third hand would be a bonus."

"Especially since yours look like the surface of a partly grated potato." She took the tube of salve and stroked it across Dani's palms and a few of her fingers.

"Ow." She had a slit in the curve of her thumb. No matter how careful the application, it stung.

"You sure none of these cuts are deep enough

to get stitched up?"

"The EMT didn't think so." She didn't mention that he had suggested she have them checked out more closely. "They'll be fine in another day or so."

Tasha finished wrapping her injuries in a thin gauze layer and retrieved a baggie of crushed ice from the freezer. "Will you be okay for a bit while I go to the gym?" She laid the ice across Dani's hands.

"I'll be fine."

Her roommate grinned and scooted out of the kitchen. Left alone with her thoughts and her ice, Dani stared at her white-wrapped hands.

I was almost killed. Would have been if the column had been any further from where she fell through. And it hadn't helped Darren Balducci at all.

Was this the way her life was going to be? One frightening death-stare after another?

If so, how did Jay Hunter, or any man for that

matter, fit into the picture?

Maybe they didn't. Is that what you're showing me, God? After what she and Jay had been through, after the way he'd so tenderly kissed her last night?

The front door opened. Tasha heading out to finish her workout. But after a goofy giggle, her roommate's voice rose. "Oh, Dani. Gotta visitor."

The sing-song of her voice revealed the guest before Dani ventured from the kitchen, still cupping the bag of ice across her palms.

Jay filled the doorway, his dark hair curling a bit over his forehead. His half-smile made her heart hop. He carried a ribbon-wrapped bouquet of yellow roses. "I hope you don't mind me coming over."

"I thought you'd be at work."

"Yeah, well, I'm on duty so much, it's hard to figure when I'm not officially at work."

She knew the feeling. "The flowers are beautiful."

"From Tyler. Right near where I grew up." He carried them into the kitchen. "You have a vase?"

"Top shelf." She leaned her head toward the corner cabinet.

"Yellow roses aren't only available in Texas, but they do have a pretty strong significance here." He filled the vase and arranged the flowers.

"There's a song, isn't there?"

"An old one." He laughed. "But I won't sing it. You've been injured enough." He set the vase on the table and glanced at her hands. "Are they all right?"

She nodded. "Scratches mostly. Sore, but only temporarily."

"Good." The tiny smile-lines at his eyes vanished, replaced with a thin crevice between his eyebrows. "I hate that you were injured. I wished I'd have put the pieces together faster."

She set the bag of ice on the cloth-covered table, next to the roses. "But you did." She laid a wrapped hand against his jacket sleeve. "You figured everything out and got to me in perfect time. I'd never have gotten down without your help."

He slid the fingertips of one hand against her cheek, stroking it with his thumb. "I'll always be here for you." His tender gaze held hers for a moment. "If you need me."

"I'll always need you, Sherlock." That was one truth she could express. She leaned in to his palm and let her gaze drift to his mouth.

A slow half-smile spread as he lingered a moment. Then it seemed to drop away as he lowered his gaze and moved to exit. "By the way, good job, Watson. I'm still ticked at you for putting yourself into danger." He opened the door and turned back. "But you are one sharp lady." He lifted her chin with his forefinger. "Nice to have you on my side."

She grinned. "I think we make a great team."

He released her chin and his smile faded. "Not that we'll be a team again anytime soon."

Ouch. A leg-wax would have been more pleasant. "Well, I know I'm not a detective. I don't expect to investigate together."

He pressed his lips together. "I'm not sure we should anything together." He shook his head. "It wouldn't be appropriate."

Huh? He started to turn away, but she stepped out and reached for him with her pathetic mitts. She couldn't even touch him. "What are you talking about?" Her volume rose.

He glanced to the parking lot then stepped back inside, ushering her as he went. He shut the door. "Look, Dani. I care about you. I do." His hand went to the back of his neck. "But I don't …." He spread his hands. "I know it's old fashioned, but when I date someone, it's exclusive. I'm not interested in playing around."

What did she do? "So … you're not interested in dating me." She made the statement, hoping the whimper she felt stayed out of her voice.

"Not as long as you're with Matthew. It just

isn't right."

"Matthew?" She stuck her chin forward. Had she heard him correctly?

"I heard your phone call."

Ugh. First Matthew makes her life impossible by dragging her to this city and dumping her without friends, family, or even personal contact. Now he was going to ruin her chances with Jay.

"Matthew isn't my boyfriend. Nothing like that." She released a laugh, though it sounded more like an irritated scoff.

"You said you needed him."

Ew. "Not like that." She shook her head. "Matthew …." How did she explain him? "He helps me with …."

"Situations." Jay shifted his weight to one leg.

"He sort of looks after me."

He lifted his head in a slow nod. "I get it. Now that your dad is gone."

Exactly. "Yes. Yes. And I always call him when I'm in trouble."

He stepped closer, his chin lowered. "Stupid of me to assume. I know better."

She closed the remains of the gap between them and laid her wrapped hands against his chest. "I hope you know that I care about you, too."

That half-smile again. Swoon. He carefully took her hands and kissed each covered palm, gazing into her eyes. Releasing one of her hands, he stroked her cheek with his thumb. He reached for her kiss, pressing lightly against her lips and lingering for a moment.

Dani breathed in his spicy essence as she returned his kiss. What she wouldn't give to remain in that moment for years.

His gentle, dark gaze scanned her face as he backed away. "I guess this means we'll attempt another date?" He laughed and pulled her door opened.

She nodded and watched him jog down the steps before she closed the door. "Anytime, Sherlock."

Excerpt from Grime Spree

Dani stared into Tonio's dark gaze.

He arched a thick eyebrow in her direction and tilted his head toward the hallway on her left labeled with the word *Salon* in a swirling font.

"I've heard everything here is outstanding." Jay turned the thick page of the menu.

Behind him, Tonio's eyes pierced her. Again, he bobbed his head toward her left. His spiked black hair quivered with the movement.

She hazarded a glance around the dining room. Were any of the *others* here? When her gaze met back with Tonio's, he'd completed pouring water at the neighboring table. His eyes were slits, and his bottom lip had rolled between his teeth.

Dani startled. It had been a year since she'd seen his particular type of silent insistence. And witnessed the repercussions of failure to obey. "I'll be right back." She could only hope. She laid her napkin across the chair cushion and picked up her purse.

The hallway lay in front of her. Though she'd lost track of Tonio, doubtless, he hadn't lost track of her. And he wouldn't hesitate to hurt Jay to force her into his will. None of the men she'd known would think twice about an ancillary casualty. Especially if that casualty were a cop.

She proceeded around a corner. A hand shot from the shadows behind a plastic ficus and clamped over her mouth, while a muscular arm wrapped around her waist. She focused on the arm, sinking her stubby nails into it and pushing against her captor, but the man only tightened his hold.

"I'm trying to help you, stupid." Tonio's whisper sounded more hiss-like than she remembered. "Settle down, Sammi. You gotta get outta here." The Brooklyn accent and the sound of her real name jolted her. She stilled, and he loosened his hold.

"What's going on?" She drew her fingers around her lips to remove the feel of his rough hand.

"Nothing you need to know about, but if you don't get out of here, and fast, someone else might see you. Someone who's not as kind as I am."

For Discussion & Study

Give me a holler if you want to set up a Skype session with your book club.
AuthorMarjiLaine@gmail.com

1. Ephesians 3:20-21 spoke to me as I contemplated this story. Dani has lost all that is dear to her and must shed areas of her personality in order to remain in hiding. So when something outstanding and beyond her imagination begins, she has trouble accepting the potential blessing. Have you ever experienced such—had trouble realizing an amazing gift from your awesome Father?

2. Along the same lines, do you remember a time, looking back, when the blessing was so much more than the request or expectation? What was your reaction?

3. Verse 21 of that section quotes: "… to Him be glory in the church …." What would (or does) that look like in your church? What can you do to insure His glory there happens or continues?

4. Dani accuses Jay of having trust issues. What is the irony with this? Have you ever trusted someone who didn't tell you the whole truth? When you realized the deception, what was the result? Were you able to make amends?

5. Some say that people who have trust issues have either been too often burned or are not very honest themselves and therefore expect duplicity in others. Have you noticed that to be the case? Do you have trouble trusting other people? Why?

6. In Matthew 10:16, Christ tells his followers to be both wise and innocent. These two almost seem antonyms. Wise sees and expects the evil activity of the world, and innocent uses rose-colored glasses. How can someone be both?

7. How trustworthy are you? When is it all right to lie and under what conditions? Ephesians 4:25 holds a key here.

8. Is Dani right to keep her secret from her new loved-ones: her own roommate Tasha, her friends Ty and Carla Reid, and especially Jay who might become someone very special? How would telling them her secret put them in danger? Should she tell them, and if so, how?

9. With Dani's secrets and her lies, does her relationship with Jay have any chance at all?

10. Near the end of this story, Cal discards his laid-back, careless manner after the suicide of teenager. His bitterness shows as he questions why God didn't stop the girl—didn't change

her mind. Anyone can see that bad things happen in the world, so Cal's frustration isn't farfetched. Have you ever struggled with his issue? Have you ever been angry with God? How would you answer him or someone else who wonders why bad things happen to good people? John 16:33

11. Jay describes God as a Father who doesn't want to force anyone to loving Him. How does John 3:16 confirm this argument? The truth is bad things do happen to good people. How can Christians, those who strive to be like Christ, cope with this truth and its opposite (good things happen to bad people)? See Psalm 37 and 73 on this topic.

12. Just for fun. Psychology, analyzing characters, is a hobby. Did Jay change at all in this story? Did Dani? What are the traits they have that will make their relationship work? Are there any hindrances, besides Dani's secrets, that will hurt their relationship?

Marji Laine writes about hope and redemption. Her characters, tangled in desperate situations, rely on authentic faith in God to carry them through treachery, betrayal, and impossible circumstances.

A "graduated" homeschooling mom of four, she now teaches a high school Bible study and aspiring authors at various workshops and writing conferences. She spends most of her time formatting and designing books for Write Integrity Press. She also helps those through Roaring Lambs Ministry tell their stories.

Living with her sweet hubby of 33 years and her two rescue dogs, Marji loves her jobs – loves writing, formatting, and building covers. But given the choice, she'd rather be laughing, playing games, or doing projects with her family where one-liners are a norm. While she enjoys recharging on her own, she loves being a little goofy with her kids and their friends or acting and singing from time to time on stage.

> *Content is probably the best description of me. I teach my kids to "enjoy where they are while they're there." A lesson in joy that I had to learn the hard way.*

She prefers mountains to beaches, dogs to cats, entrees to desserts, and Jaguars to any other vehicle. Her favorites include emerald green, autumn, stargazer lilies and white roses, New York style pizza, and red velvet cake with cream cheese icing.

You can keep up with Marji by joining her monthly newsletter list at her website, www.MarjiLaine.com. And you can also find her at the WriteIntegrity.com website as well as on her Facebook Page.

Dear Reader,

I'm so glad you used your valuable time reading Grime Wave. My hope is that the truths about our Heavenly Father that are embedded in this story will remind you of how dear you are to Him.

As I read through some of the discussions, like the part where Jay is trying to help Cal get through his bitterness, the Spirit inside me shouts, "Amen." The Father dotes on us and craves our devotion, but He wants our free will intact when we come to Him.

I'm reminded of how Jesus describes it in Revelation 3:20, "I stand at the door and knock; if anyone hears My voice and opens the door, I will come in ...." He doesn't pick the lock of the door. Neither does He kick it down. We have to invite Him inside.

I'm praying for you, dear reader, that your heart will be touched and your spirit strengthened.

If you enjoyed *Grime Wave*, I hope that you will return to its Amazon page and leave a review of about twenty-five words and hopefully five stars. And while you're there, download *Grime Beat*, the first book of the Grime Fighter Series.

Stick around Faith Driven Fiction for more information about Dani and Jay. There might even be a short story or two until the next two books can come out.

I'm so delighted with this second episode of the Grime Fighter series. As with the first story, Jennifer Slattery and Carole Towriss were pivotal in the development of Dani's character and the relationship between her and Jay. Even my sweet hubby got involved in the plotting this time. And the story is so much better for their help. Patricia Pacjac Carroll and Jackie Castle encouraged me to go deeper into my characters. The final polish, given by Christa Upton, and my wonderful cover model, Emily Gibbons, made *Grime Wave* shine.

Again, my family has offered exceptional support. My girls never let me quit. I'm so grateful for their encouragement. The Lord blesses me so much through them. And I also thank Him for the words He chooses to share with me. I pray I can continue to be faithful to His direction and walking in His way.

Until next time, dear reader!

Be Blessed!

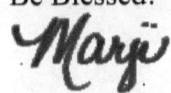

Other Books from Marji Laine

Grime Fighter Mysteries
A Complete Series!

Working as a crime scene cleaner is perfect for neat-nick Dani Foster who has recently been relocated by her witness security contact. But she can't hide the investigative reactions drilled into her by her detective father. Even though her discoveries, and the explorations they instigate, often put her into funny, uncomfortable, and sometimes dangerous positions.

Marji Laine

Heath's Point Suspense
COUNTER POINT – Book 1

Her dad's gone. Her business is in trouble, and her car's in the lake. Cat McPHerson doesn't have anything else to lose... except her life. And a madman is determined to take that.

Her former boyfriend, Ray Alexander, returns as a hero from his foreign mission, bringing back death-threats. Cat must find a way to trust Ray, the man who broke her heart or neither of them will survive.

BREAKING POINT – Book 2

Why would anyone want her dead?

Alynne Stone wanted nothing to do with her parents' inn after they left their lifelong home in Dallas to move to Heath's Point, Texas. Then an emergency phone call not only drew her to her parents' bed and breakfast, it thrust her into the crosshairs of a killer.

Lieutenant Jason Danvers has no idea why his kind and generous friend was killed. But the man's beautiful, prodigal daughter needs all the help he can give her to stay alive.

AIN'T MISBEHAVING

Book 1 of the
Dallas Duets Clean Billionaire Romance Series

Annalee Chambers: Poised, wealthy, socially elite.
Convict.

She floated through life in a pampered, crystal bubble until she smashed it with a single word. Dealing with the repercussions of that word might break her, ruin her family, and land her in jail. That is, unless a handsome worker from the "other" side of the tracks, who has secrets of his own, can help her find her way.

You'll most often find Marji either writing or editing in her favorite recliner with her rescue dogs at her feet. Or you can look for her at: MarjiLaine.com, Facebook.com/MarjiLaine, or at her author page on Amazon.

www.ingramcontent.com/pod-product-compliance
Lightning Source LLC
Chambersburg PA
CBHW020322200626
46814CB00006BB/2366